kill devil hills

kill devil hills

Sarah Darlington

_To Denise –
Happy reading!
Sarah Darlington_

KILL DEVIL HILLS

Cover Design by Perfect Pear Creative Covers
Editing by Editing 4 Indies
Find Sarah online:
www.facebook.com/sarahdarlingtonauthor

To my younger sister, Laura. For always being there for me no matter what.

chapter 1

NOAH

I had to take a piss. It had been a hard day—not the hardest of my life, but right up there. Ellie and I had gotten wasted to make up for it. And now both of us had to use the bathroom at the exact same moment.

"I hhhhhave ta use the pisser, too. Ladies first," Ellie announced, standing up from the coffee table and leaving our two person game of *Taboo*. It was something we often played after a long night of drinking, and tonight we'd especially needed something routine. "You men have it easy. You have bigger bladders."

"Don't kid yourself," I joked. "You're just as much of a man as I am."

She laughed before feigning seriousness. "Shut up, Noah," she said, swaying as she moved for the bathroom.

Ellie was a lightweight, as much as she liked to pretend she wasn't, and I moved after her in hopes that I'd save her from wobbling into the wall. My attempt was useless, because by the time I stood to my feet, she'd already disappeared into the bathroom. And by this point, all this talk about peeing had me really needing to go now. So I marched up the stairs, heading for one of the other bathrooms.

The Turner's house had three levels, and in my drunken stupor I ended up all the way upstairs. *How the hell did that happen?* Ellie's parents and two sisters must have gone to bed hours ago, because it was dead quiet upstairs. The kind of dead quiet that made my skin crawl and left an unsettled feeling in the pit of my stomach. Years ago, Memaw—the grandmother who had raised me for a time—told me that after a person passes away their soul lingers for a few days. Who knew if that was true or not? And what sort of woman told an eight-year-old about 'lingering souls?' But all I could think about was Ben's soul lingering in this very hallway as I crept for the bathroom, the floorboards squeaking under my shoes. The bathroom door was closed, thankfully not locked, and I stumbled inside. Light blinded me before my eyes started to adjust.

"Jesus. Lord. Fuck."

Blood *everywhere.*

In an instant, I went sober. The sight before me was beyond horrific. Serious slasher movie shit. *Was someone fucking murdered in here?* Because all I could see was red, contrasting sharply against white tile. Then my eyes finished adjusting, and I realized that Ellie's younger sister Georgina had slit her wrists. Well, not just her wrists. It looked like she'd slit her whole fucking arm. Both of them. There was way too much blood to know for sure. Her body was slumped, propped up against the side of the tub, while her arms were turned up as if she were meditating with her eyes peacefully shut.

Dropping straight to my knees, I yelled her name and for help. My voice sounded shrill, barely recognizable as my own. Terrified she might already be dead, I brushed her long brown hair away from her neck and felt for a pulse.

She had one, a faint one, but it was there.

Thank Christ!

Common sense told me I needed to slow the blood flow. And by the way she'd dug into her arms with the big-ass kitchen knife on the tile floor beside her, I knew that wasn't going to be easy. I moved her body flat on the floor and pulled her legs up to rest on my lap. Blood stained everything. Yanking my shirt over my head, I ripped at the fabric and tied the pieces around her arms. It wasn't enough. I used my hands to put pressure on the cuts. By this time, Mr. and Mrs. Turner were awake and in the bathroom, yelling frantic things at me while they called 911. But I pushed out the noise and the ringing in my ears, focusing all my attention on her.

Amongst the chaos, her blue eyes flickered open for a single, brief moment and hope shook through my body. Her eyes were glazed-over and distant but managed to connect with mine.

"Noah, I'm cold," she whispered, before her lids fluttered closed once more.

"You will *not* die on me," I told her with absolute certainty. "I won't let you." I leaned over to press my chest against her body, hoping that might keep her warmer. Then I did the one thing I never thought I'd do again—I prayed to God. He'd let me down a few too many times, and we weren't on speaking terms these days, but I'd never needed anything more. I begged. I pleaded. And then the next thing I knew, the paramedics were there, taking her away from me. I asked them frantic questions, needing to know if she would live, but my questions went unanswered, time and everyone moving faster than my foggy brain could keep up with.

I blinked.

Georgie was gone.

Ellie stood in the bathroom with me now. I hadn't moved from my spot on the ground, and Ellie yanked on my arm, trying unsuccessfully to pull me to my feet.

"Go with them to the hospital," I insisted. "I'm fine."

"Noah, you're covered in blood. Get up."

"No."

"Well, I can't go to the hospital. Mom went in the ambulance, and Dad already left. I'm too drunk to drive, and someone had to stay here with

Rose. I think you're in shock. You need to get up."

Glancing up, I took in the sight of my best friend. She had black stuff streaked down her cheeks and some of Georgie's blood smeared in her spikey brown hair. Ellie was tough. She never cried. It hurt my already churning stomach to see her so upset—especially seeing it for the second time today. "I'm not in shock," I assured her. "I'm fine. Go take care of Rose. Don't let her near this bathroom. She's too little to see something this fucked up. Let me know when you know anything new about Georgie. In the meantime, I'm going to try to clean some of this."

"You don't have to do that." She wiped her nose on her sleeve, shaking noticeably.

"Yes, I do. You know how I get."

She nodded, reluctant but agreeing. "Okay. I'll go get you some towels and bleach. Thanks, Noah." She went for the door.

"For cleaning? I have nothing better to do right now."

"No, for saving her life. The paramedic said if you'd found her even a few minutes later or hadn't done all you did…she'd be—" She sighed a big huff of air and continued, "She'd be dead now, too. You saved her."

I'd never saved anyone or anything in my whole life. I didn't like the idea of it. I was nobody's hero. But the alternative option would have been to let Georgie die, so I guess just this once an exception had to be made.

Ellie left and returned a few minutes later with towels, bleach, and cleaning supplies. I might have known I needed to get Georgie flat on the floor and elevate her legs when that had mattered, but I didn't have the first clue on how to clean up a giant bloody mess. Once I started, I realized the smell of blood and bleach didn't mix well, and all I'd done was spread the red further over the tile floor. My cleaning wasn't helping jack. *Dammit.* I sighed, taking a step backward, trying to come up with a better plan to tackle the mess. That was when I noticed a pink cellphone lying rather ominously on the bathroom sink. Georgie's cellphone.

Being nosy as hell and not caring, I grabbed it and slid the unlock button to turn on the screen. The notes app on the phone opened. She'd left a goodbye letter. It read:

I'm sorry. I know my timing is horrible, but I couldn't let Ben go into the dark alone. He's my other half. Please understand. I love you all, but I love him, too. And now I'm with him. Love, tons and tons of love, Georgina

It was the sweetest and the stupidest fucking note I'd ever read. She'd lost her brother. Watching his casket being lowered into the ground was hard for all of us to watch today. I understood she was in pain. I understood she wanted to ease that pain. She wanted to follow him into the dark… I even understood that. What I didn't understand was why it was cutting me up inside. Because it was. Finding her on that floor, holding her cold body, watching as the paramedics took her away, and staring at the evidence of it all still staining the bathroom floor—it was ripping me to fucking shreds. And it had been years since I'd let something affect me like this.

"Noah—" Ellie came rushing back into the bathroom. "Dad just called."

"Tell me she'll live," I demanded.

"She's gonna live."

I let out a breath of air I hadn't realized I'd been holding in.

chapter **2:**

FOUR MONTHS LATER

GEORGINA

There comes a time in every person's life when they hit rock bottom. And it is how you handle yourself when that time comes that defines you. It was safe to say, when my rock bottom came screaming in my face, I'd failed. Miserably. I had tried to commit suicide—*tried* being the operative word in that statement. If it hadn't been for my sister's friend, Noah Clark, then I'd be dead. The most depressing part of all, I still wasn't one hundred percent sure if Noah saving me was a good thing.

But, nevertheless, he *had* saved me. Maybe I was still trying to figure out how to be okay. Maybe I was still missing my brother every single moment of the day. And maybe I was still nothing close to the person I wanted to be. But I had a smidgeon of hope now, where before I'd thought I had none, and I had Noah to thank for that.

I sighed, staring out the window at the rows and rows of beach houses ticking by. The Cove—the recovery facility I'd been sent to and had spent the last four months 'recovering' at—was a three hour drive from our seaside home in Kill Devil Hills, North Carolina. Four months and three hours had flown by, and we were minutes away from the house. It had been an uncomfortable drive, given that my parents had forgotten how to act normal around me, and I feared being home and facing reality again.

I guess I feared it all because I'd loved The Cove so much. It was a residential treatment center for young women suffering from anything from drug addiction to eating disorders, which focused on building skills for the future. Pure 'let's-hold-hands-and-sing-Kumbaya' bullcrap, but surprisingly I'd fit in rather well there. Before Ben's death, I'd been so caught up in my own little world of friends, parties, and my boyfriend, that I hadn't even noticed how wildly unhappy I was until it was too late. Take me out of that world and I'd done shockingly well. But put me back into my old world—what if everything just came crashing down on me all over again? What if I wasn't strong enough to exist in my old world?

"Ellie's making dinner," Mom announced. She'd run out of random things to chat about two hours ago.

"Oh," I answered.

Mom continued on, talking to me in a sweet, soft, careful voice. "I wanted to have a nice family dinner tonight. I wanted it waiting for you when we arrived home. Ellie volunteered."

Ellie's cooking would probably be disastrous, but that actually sounded better than whatever overly-healthy, latest-diet-trend dinner my mom might have fixed instead.

"I'm sure it will be great," I replied politely, but my heart was now pounding just a little harder than it should have been. Because if Ellie was at home, then Noah Clark would surely be there with her.

Noah was my sister's best friend. They went to high school together, graduated together, decided to forego college together to start their own business, and currently lived together. The two were pretty damn inseparable. And if my sister wasn't a lesbian, I'd have assumed the next step in their undying friendship would be marriage and babies. But my older sister liked girls, and Noah was just her really good friend. Her really *good-looking* good friend. Her really good-looking good friend who saved my life and now kept creeping into my thoughts at random moments like now…

A second later, Dad pulled into the driveway of our house. A.k.a. 'The Shore Thing.' It was standard around here to name your house and to post that name like a name-tag over the front door on a wooden placard. The neighbor's house to the right was called 'Beachy Keen.' And to the left sat a vacation rental by the name of 'Sol Mate.' Kind of cheesy, but the tourists seemed to like the different names. Or at least that was what Dad was always saying. He was a realtor so I guess he would know.

Dad grabbed my luggage, Mom grabbed her purse, and I fidgeted with the hem of my long-sleeved shirt. It was early June, already hot as balls in North Carolina, but I had on jeans and a long-sleeved shirt because razors at The Cove had been banned, and I desperately needed to shave...everywhere. Not to mention, I liked long sleeves since they were good at hiding my scars.

I pushed open the front door, entering the house through the lower level. Basements were impossible this close to the ocean, but in all practicality, the lower level *was* our basement. It had Ellie's old room, a guest room, a bathroom, and a game room. I took the stairs two at a time, leaving my parents behind—no sense in delaying the awkward-ass meet-and-greet coming my way—and headed for the main level. That was where the kitchen, living room, and all my other family members would be. It was also where Noah would be. Might as well get that nerve-racking, thanks-for-saving-my-life-even-though-I-didn't-want-to-be-saved, did-I-mention-I-can't-stop-thinking-about-you-lately weird moment over with as well.

But the only person I found was my little sister, Rose. She was sitting on the couch, watching some pointless reality TV show. She gave me a menacing glare from across the room when I entered, and then resumed watching whatever she was watching. *Okay? What was her problem? She was nine for crying out loud but acting like a moody teenager.*

"Hi, Rose."

She flipped her long, chocolate-colored hair over one shoulder. "Hi, yourself."

"Aren't you going to give me a hug? I haven't seen you for almost four months."

"Nope."

BEEEEEP! BEEEEEP! BEEEEEEEEEP!

Just then the smoke alarm went off in the kitchen. Oh God, Mom never should have left the cooking up to Ellie. The smell of burning hit my nose just as I heard my older sister shout, "Shit! Noah, get the fire extinguisher!"

Jeez! I plopped down on the couch by Rose rather than dealing with that. Mom, surely hearing the commotion from all the way downstairs with her mom-hearing, hurried through the living room a second later and dropped her purse on the floor as she rushed to help out in the kitchen. The next thing I knew, Ellie—with Noah following close behind her—came laughing out into the living room like they'd both just been banished by Mom. She and Noah had little specks of white stuff all over them.

"That was hella awesome!" Ellie was saying. "Who knew macaroni and cheese could catch on fire like that?" She grabbed Noah's shirt dramatically. "Noah Clark, you're my hero."

From the couch, I watched them—neither had noticed me yet. Once, a few years back, I heard one of Ellie's girlfriends refer to her as, "butch in the streets, femme in the sheets." I was not sure what that meant, if it had been a compliment or not, but I took it as…Ellie sure looked the part of a masculine lesbian—all macho and swagger, short hair and tattoos—but deep down she was a sweetheart. Kind, caring, and loving. As for Noah…well, no point in denying it, the guy was all man.

His golden, sun-bleached hair was just long enough to tie back haphazardly into a ponytail at the nape of his neck, little pieces always falling loose. He had brown eyes and a strong jawline, rivaling someone like Brad Pitt. Sometimes he shaved, but not today. His shoulders were wide enough to fill a door and I had a fleeting image—one scarred on my cortex—of the way his muscular chest looked shirtless. *Holy hell!* The guy was a delicious cross between a California surfer, a mountain man, and Thor, and I tried to keep my eyes glued on the TV. Really, I did. But still, my cheeks burned, and my wild, ridiculous thoughts would not stop. I'd been hoping that seeing him in person after four months would squash these unwanted feelings. Maybe being locked away at an all-girls facility caused me to over-glorify and hype him up to more than he was. But nope. Noah Clark was just as striking in person as he was in all my late-night fantasies.

Crap on a crap-stick. I dug my fingernails into my jeans. He and Ellie still hadn't noticed me sitting there, and I didn't want to be blushing or hyperventilating when they did.

I'd always found Noah to be attractive, even during his high-school emo/Goth phase when his hair was dyed black and he wore combat boots in the summer. But I'd never seriously considered him, because truthfully, I'd been a little scared (and a lot intimidated) of the guy. He was almost six years older than me and not much of a talker. He had the whole brooding 'I-hate-the-world' thing down perfectly. But that same tormented oddball had also done everything in his power to save my life when it had mattered most. So yeah…now, and over the past few months, I suddenly found myself seriously considering him. I wanted to know who Noah Clark really was. *What did my sister know that the rest of the world didn't?*

To make my insane crush worse, I still technically, kinda-sorta had a boyfriend. Logan Tyler. We hadn't spoken in almost four months, but we hadn't officially broken up yet either. That would be corrected soon, but still. Either way, I shouldn't have been thinking about Noah in any capacity, especially when he was standing six feet away from me.

"Hello. Earth to Georgie!" Ellie called out, pulling me out of my thoughts and back into the present. She was the last person on the planet to still call me Georgie and that used to bother me, but as she bear-tackled me against the couch—the first person to hug me this tight in months—I found myself wondering why I used to always fight her so much on something as stupid as a name. She tickled me until I was crying 'uncle,' then she let up. "It's good to have you home, kiddo. Did Mom make you want to slit your wrists all over again on the drive home?"

The smallest exhale of air came from Noah, a sound I might have missed if Ellie hadn't reacted immediately to it.

"What?" she asked him, as if he'd managed to shock her. She turned around on the couch to face where he stood. "Is it too soon for jokes, Mr. Sensitive? Lighten up, Georgie's fine."

He didn't answer her, but his eyes found mine. He gave me a simple look, one that likely meant nothing, but my heart slammed inside my chest nonetheless. And for a fraction of a second, it was as if the two of us shared something the rest of the world didn't have privilege to. I had no idea what the hell that something was, and it didn't matter anyway, because my small moment with Noah evaporated as fast as it began. His face turned expressionless as his gaze shifted to Rose's TV program.

"Okay," Mom shouted from the kitchen. "Dinner's ready. Everybody go sit so we can eat."

Ellie gave my knee a little squeeze, staying behind with me on the couch for a moment as everyone else went to sit around the dining room table. "I shouldn't be worried about you, right? Or *was* it too soon for jokes?" she whispered, being serious for once in her life.

I shrugged. "I don't know, but I like how you've treated me normally since everything happened."

She nodded, looking sullen for exactly one second before a wicked grin filled her face. "This is going to be the best freaking summer of your life," she whispered, excitement in her voice. "You're eighteen now. You're finally done with stupid high school. You can do whatever the hell you want—except drink, but that's just a technicality—and I'm going to make it my personal mission this summer to ensure that every single day you wake up regretting taking that knife to your pretty skin. Just stick with me and Noah, and you'll learn that the world can bend if you need it to. Rule Number One: There are no rules. Nothing is black and white."

I gulped. I had no idea what she was talking about, and honestly, it kind of scared the crap out of me. But for the way she was smiling, I wanted to trust whatever it was she was saying. And if sticking with her meant sticking with Noah, how was I supposed to turn down that small opportunity?

"Sure," I answered, "I could do that."

"Good. Now come and try my macaroni and cheese. I microwaved the pasta before I cooked it. It's supposed to make it better. Except the recipe never called for it to catch on fire…so I'm hoping that just added more flavor."

I couldn't help but smile. One of the things I learned at The Cove was to gravitate toward the 'real' people in my life—the people who would love and support me no matter what. To lean on them, trust in them, confide in them, and let them become an 'ally' to me. Before Ben's death, I hadn't given my family any of my love. I'd saved it all up for my friends at school, Logan, and the things I used to think mattered. Ellie and I had never been very close, at least not during my teenage years, because I'd never given her much of a chance. She was a lesbian, with a crazy amount of tattoos, and had a best friend who looked like he belonged in a motorcycle gang—hanging out with her would have been social suicide. No pun intended. But I vowed right then, that I would never again judge my sister based on those things. And I wouldn't stand by and listen when others judged her based on those things anymore either.

I sat down at the table, purposely avoiding glancing in Noah's direction because he only made breathing difficult, and loaded a heaping pile of Ellie's macaroni onto my plate. It had some white flakes in it that probably came from the fire extinguisher, but I spooned a giant bite into my mouth anyway.

"This is amazing," I said, because surprisingly it was. "Best welcome home meal ever, Ellie."

She laughed and took my compliment.

* * *

The rest of the meal passed okay...and by *okay* I mean boring and awkward. Ellie and Mom had a tendency to argue and neither spoke, probably both trying to make an effort for me. I actually wouldn't have minded if they'd argued, because that would have felt more normal than the silence. Then there was Rose. She sat through the entire dinner with earbuds in. It shocked the hell out of me that neither of my parents made her take them out. Noah was Noah—quiet like usual. And Dad...well, he tried really hard to make conversation. He spoke first about the warm weather and then about some of the vacation rentals he managed. But no one took the bait and joined his conversation, and soon he gave up. The silence was deafening.

The problem for me was...the last time we'd had a big family dinner like this was when Ben had been alive. I'd had four months to come to grips with my brother's death, and it still hurt like hell. But I never anticipated how excruciating it would be to do normal things like this without him. Well, even if he were still alive, the odds were that he wouldn't have been having dinner with us and at this table anyway, but I hated knowing he wasn't having dinner anywhere in the world right now. The enthusiasm I'd felt with Ellie minutes ago faded as fast as she'd created it. I quickly finished the rest of my meal. Even Noah's good looks weren't enough to distract away my heavy heart.

"This meal was great," I told everyone and the silent room. "I think I'm going to go unpack. If that's okay?" They all stared at me as I stood up. Even Noah.

"Okay," Mom answered. "A new Netflix movie came in the mail yesterday. I figured we could all watch it together in a little while. What do you think?"

"Sure," I said, appeasing her as fast as possible so I could leave the room. I took my plate to the sink, rinsing it and putting it in the dishwasher, and then hurried upstairs to my room. I needed to unpack.

And to cry.

chapter **3:**

NOAH

I couldn't make sense of Georgie's happy demeanor and then her sudden need to leave the dinner table. Whatever. I reminded myself that my fixation on her well-being could end right the fuck now. The girl was still currently breathing—the proof right in front of my eyes. So I could stop worrying and stressing liked I'd been doing non-stop over the last few months.

I still had flashbacks of that night. I'd been through shittier things in my life, but somehow the images of her lifeless body and slit wrists would not stop haunting me. It was annoying and frustrating. I hoped now that she was home I'd improve. Because, in all seriousness, it was just plain pissing me off at this point, and I wanted my regular life to resume.

On the upside of things, the girl did look healthier—color in her cheeks, and if I wasn't mistaken, a few extra pounds on her hips. Georgie had always been too damn skinny. But, despite her loose jeans and oversized long-sleeve shirt, the little extra weight looked unexpectedly good on her. It gave my chest a weird expanding sensation that I wasn't quite used to feeling. She was a beautiful girl, no mistaking that, and I assured myself that the feeling in my chest was a natural reaction any warm-blooded male would experience in her presence. It meant nothing. Less than nothing.

I focused on eating dinner and when that was over, I followed Ellie to her old room on the lower level. Her room was decked out in twinkle lights, as it had been for as long as I'd known her, and it gave everything a psychedelic feel. She plopped down on her swivel chair beside her desk and spun in a full circle. "So—bad news. I need you to fire Patrick tomorrow."

"What?" I sat on the edge of her bed, resting my elbows on my knees. "Why?"

She avoided eye contact, turning another full circle. "He stole from the cash register. I caught him in the act."

Grabbing the chair's arm rests, I put a stop to her incessant spinning and forced her to look in my direction. "What the hell, Ellie? Why didn't *you* fire him the moment it happened?"

"I wanted to—seriously, I did. But Patrick gave me the saddest puppy-dog eyes. I couldn't do it. I need you to be the bad cop. I'm the good cop."

"We aren't cops."

Now Ellie gave me sad puppy-dog eyes and the cutest frown crossed her pink lips. I was such a sucker when it came to this girl. I'd do anything for her, as I know she'd do for me, and I couldn't help but give in.

"Fuck. Fine. I'll do it tomorrow."

Ellie stood up and playfully flung her arms around my neck. "I love you, Noah Clark. You're too good to me."

"Yeah, yeah." I smiled, letting her hug me for a small second before peeling her arms off me. "Let's go watch whatever Netflix movie your mom got in the mail for tonight."

"Really?" she asked, her eyes searching my face for something she wasn't going to find. "You know, it's probably a chick-flick or something equally lame. You don't have to stay. I'm going to, but it's cool if you want to leave."

I didn't mind staying, and she already knew that. Any other day, 'pre-Georgie-incident,' she wouldn't have questioned me either. I'd never had the warm, loving, *Leave it to Beaver* family that she did. I had a shitty one instead. And when Ellie and I became friends, way back in the ninth grade, and she found out about my jacked-up home life, she'd automatically shared her family with me. She was only questioning me right now because of the timing and because I'd asked about her sister a few too many times over the last four months. *But so fucking what if I was concerned for Georgie and wanted to stay at her house a little longer because of that? So fucking what?*

"Nah, I want to stay," I told Ellie.

"Okay." She shrugged, letting it go as quickly as she'd brought it up. "Whatever. Dibs on the recliner."

"Not if I get there first." I sprang for the bedroom door and then for the stairs. Ellie was small, but fast and never one to back down from a challenge. She chased after me. We were neck-and-neck, rushing up the stairs, but the moment we reached the top, both of us mellowed and our fun died. Even after four months, the somber atmosphere from Ben's death still lingered in the Turner house. I knew Ellie was sad over what happened to Ben, and also everything with Georgie, but my friend was the most optimistic person on the planet, and I could also tell she was ready to be happy again. The problem was her family was still tangled deep in the grieving process. Or at least that was the impression I got.

Ellie graciously let me have the recliner, while she took a seat on the couch by Rose. Mr. and Mrs. Turner passed out little bowls of popcorn and occupied the loveseat together. We were waiting on Georgie to join us, but she never did. And that bothered me. This whole 'caring thing' was new to me and that bothered me too. I mean, obviously I cared for Ellie and so by default I cared for her family, but I wasn't used to the protectiveness I felt for Georgie. *What the fuck?* I thought having her home would end my worrying. So far it had only doubled it.

Mrs. Turner left the room to go check on her. And almost as quickly as she disappeared, she returned. "Georgina's sleeping," she explained, her voice light but the lines on her brow became more pronounced as she spoke. "Why don't you go ahead and start the movie, Wade? I think I'm going to get some shut-eye myself. It's getting late and the six hours we spent in the car is getting to me."

Wade Turner was a strange and complicated man. He often said contradictory things at inopportune moments, spoke an octave louder than most, and his jokes were about as dry as Ellie's macaroni and cheese. For years I'd been certain he hated me. But after saving his daughter's life, I'd learned otherwise. We'd had a heart-to-heart, in this very room, where he'd thanked me and hugged me, and I think I understood him a little better now. His sarcasm was hard to read and often came across as insincere, but he loved his children fiercely…and that now included me. *You're the only son I have left,* he'd told me. *And I appreciate the love you have for this family.*

"Goodnight," Mr. Turner told his wife, stealing a quick kiss from her before she headed off to bed. Then the man heaved a giant sigh, squatted down on his hands and knees, and started fiddling around with the DVD player as if he were busy changing a car tire. A moment later (after a thorough explanation from Rose) he managed to get the movie started. Ellie had been right; it was a chick movie. But frankly, I didn't give a shit. I wasn't paying attention anyway.

The movie dragged on and eventually ended. Goodnights were said. Ellie and I headed downstairs. We didn't discuss it, but I took the bed in the spare room and decided I'd be spending the night. Crashing here wasn't out of the norm, (though typically I did it after a night of drinking) and this felt like the right place to be somehow. The guest bed was a waterbed. As outdated as that sounded, I liked it. I crawled in under the covers, settling into the middle of the squishy mattress, and hoped for an easy night's sleep. No such luck. I tossed and turned, and had all but given up on getting some shut-eye, when I heard the faint sound of water running. I heard it coming from the downstairs bathroom. *Was Ellie taking a shower at this hour?* The girl was unpredictable so probably.

After a solid twenty minutes, I came to the conclusion that there was no chance in hell it was Ellie showering—not for this long. Finally, the water stopped. I lay unmoving, listening desperately for any sound. Nothing. I listened harder. Still, nothing. And then the door to my room creaked opened suddenly. Fuck.

It wasn't Ellie. That was for damn certain.

It was Georgie.

My eyes were semi-adjusted to the darkness and apparently hers were not. Because her figure, outlined just vaguely in moonlight, hair wet and dressed in loose pajamas, snuck into my room. The door closed softly behind her, and she unknowingly sat down on top of me. Her body made contact with mine for a mere fraction of a second before she jumped away as if I'd electrocuted her, disappearing into the shadows of the room.

"Hello?" she yelped. "Who's there?"

"Georgie, it's me," I said as gently as possible, trying not to scare her further.

"Oh," she exhaled. It was a soft sound, but loud against the quiet night. "Sorry. I didn't know you were here. I didn't mean to wake you up."

"You didn't wake me. Are you okay?"

I'd known her since she was a kid, and we'd never had a one-on-one conversation like this before. I couldn't even see her face, but for some unexplainable reason my heart was racing.

She was hardly that little kid anymore.

"I'm okay," she answered. "It's just…I didn't want to sleep upstairs.

I'm sorry. I'll leave."

Swinging my legs over the edge of the bed, I stood up so fast I nearly gave myself whiplash. "No. You sleep here. I can sleep out on the couch." I didn't give her a chance to protest as I speedily left the room, the sweet scent of her shampoo filling my nostrils as I hurried past her. Before she could stop me, I shut the door behind me.

The table lamp had been left on and the light blinded my unadjusted eyes. I turned it off and then made myself comfortable (or rather, uncomfortable) on the couch. My legs were a good two feet longer than the damn thing and no blankets could be found—but I was too confused by my brief conversion with Georgie to care. *She didn't want to sleep upstairs?* I guess I understood that. Her dead brother's room and the bathroom she tried to commit suicide in were upstairs. I wouldn't want to be up there either. But why was my heart still racing?

After a few minutes the pounding slowed and exhaustion washed over me. This day had been strange, the last half hour stranger, but I finally started to drift off to sleep. Except, the moment I did, Georgie's voice cut across the room—startling me all over again.

"Noah," she called softly, my name sounding *different* coming from her. "I'll never sleep knowing you're out here on that tiny couch. Trade me, please."

"No," I told her firmly. I might be a lot of things, but I sure as fuck wasn't about to make a girl sleep on this couch.

She didn't go back into the room. "Seriously. Please."

"No," I repeated, hoping I didn't sound like an asshole. "If we trade, then I wouldn't sleep."

"Then…" Her voice faltered but after a long pause she finished her thought. "Then maybe you should share with me. It's a big bed. I don't mind. And I'll stay on my side—promise."

What?! Good sense told me not to move, but that was not what happened. I stood. My feet carried me across the room and briskly past her before I could even comprehend what I was doing. She silently followed. I knew nothing was going to happen, but this sure wasn't how I ever expected to spend my night. Through the dark grayness I watched her move for the right side of the bed.

"No, I have to have that side. Take the left," I told her even though my insides were now screaming with apprehension. *Seriously, what the fuck was I getting myself into?*

She didn't argue and moved for the other side of the bed. Meanwhile, I felt around on the ground for my t-shirt. I'd tossed it aside when I'd gone to bed, only wearing the wife-beater shirt I had on underneath, and that suddenly felt like not enough clothing. I found it and yanked it over my head. Then I crawled under the covers on the right side.

The waterbed was a king. She was miles away.

"Goodnight, Noah," she whispered. "And sorry."

Did she mean sorry for this sleeping arrangement or sorry for something more? I couldn't ask. "Goodnight," I simply said.

As awkward as I might have thought this would be, I was surprised to find it wasn't. The opposite, actually. As we both lay still for a few minutes, listening to each other breathing and not sleeping, I began feeling ten times more settled than I'd ever felt over the last four months. *What a nice, fucking change.* That worrying thing I couldn't seem to stop doing...well, it stopped.

Before I knew it, I was fast asleep.

chapter 4

GEORGINA

Wow. This was exhilarating—Noah and I in *the same freaking bed!* Unfortunately enough, my Knight in Shining Armor had fallen asleep at record speed only moments ago. One second I'd heard practically no sound coming from him and the next his breaths turned long and heavy. Go figure. I rolled my eyes at the ceiling.

After dinner, when I'd gone upstairs to my room, everything looked exactly the same—the same floral comforter I'd had for years, the same photos of all my friends plastered on my closet door, and the same breathtaking ocean view out my window. I was not sure why, but despite all the 'same', somehow everything was vastly different. I felt out of place in my own room and the sensation was very unsettling. Even worse, I couldn't even bring myself to enter my bathroom. Mom had mentioned that I could start using her bathroom instead, but it felt weird too. I'd focused on unpacking, surprised that the tears that had been threatening me at dinner wouldn't fall, and feigned sleep when Mom came upstairs to check on me.

It wasn't until after eleven that the house quieted and everyone had gone to bed. That was when I'd snuck downstairs to shower. Somehow the downstairs felt much more comforting than the third floor of our house, and after my shower, I couldn't bring myself to return to my room. I never would have guessed that Noah (and I'm assuming Ellie in her room next door) had decided to stay the night. Almost lying down on top of him had been the shock of the century. I wasn't complaining though, as I was pretty positive that that small moment had been the highlight of my sucktastic year, but that didn't erase the invisible line cutting down the center of the bed. Even if he were awake, I knew Noah would never dare cross said line.

He'd been curt with me—answering my questions with as few words as possible. Not to mention, the way he'd desperately searched for his shirt. I could read his signals loud and clear— no hanky-panky. Ever. I tried not to let that hurt my feelings. The reality was he probably only saw me as the broken little girl he'd found bleeding on a bathroom floor. Maybe this scenario was different than all my late-night fantasies, but still, it was better than nothing. And when I finally fell asleep, I fell asleep with a smile on my face. I felt safe with Noah.

Morning came way too fast. I would have liked more time to linger in my dreams, but Ellie's booming voice woke me up bright and early. "Noah, dammit, wake up! We're gonna be late—*again!*" she yelled. It was Sunday. Where could they possibly have to go? Church? Ellie then proceeded to beat her fist against the guest bedroom door as hard as she could.

I thought for sure she was about to barge in and find me in bed with him. When that didn't happen, I rubbed the sleep from my eyes and dared my first peek over at Noah. Despite Ellie's racket, he was still out of it. He slept on his stomach, his tan and impressive biceps wrapped under the pillow that his face was buried deep into. *When did a guy who owned and operated a miniature golf place have the time to work out?* I didn't know—one of a million things I didn't know. Aside from a few basic facts I knew about him, it occurred to me that we were basically strangers.

"Seriously, Noah!" came Ellie's voice again. "You need to start setting your cell phone alarm. This shit is getting old!"

I figured I couldn't lie here forever staring at the guy while my sister screamed. So I reached out to nudge his arm. The moment my fingers made contact with his skin he muttered, "I hear her."

"Oh." Jolted by his words, I quickly pulled my hand back over to my side. *How long had he been awake?*

"Maybe if I ignore her she'll go away," he said, surprising me again by speaking. His voice was rough and scratchy yet held an unexpected warmth to it. He shifted and his whiskey-colored eyes, a prettier brown than I'd ever been close enough to notice, connected with mine. "Nah," he decided. "Not possible for Ellie."

I didn't have a response for that. He'd only said a few words, but I was beyond shocked he was even talking to me. We'd never talked more than this. All I could do was lie there and try desperately to play it cool. But the intimacy of sharing a bed and the easiness of his eyes on mine had my heart pounding in my ears, practically bursting my eardrums.

Too bad Ellie broke our tiny moment when she continued to beat on the door. "Noah!"

Noah had no choice but to finally answer her. "Let up, woman," he called out to her. "I'm awake. You don't have to break down the door."

"Whatever, Noah," she huffed. "I'm going upstairs for a Pop-Tart. Get your ass out of bed and shower so we can go. I do this shit for you." Her words were followed by the stomping of her feet up the stairs.

Holy smokes. Noah and I were now completely alone! I didn't really know how to handle that and said the first thing that burst into my head. "You two argue like an old married couple. It's kinda cute."

He merely shrugged and pushed himself out of the bed. Gathering what appeared to be his wallet, keys, and phone off the bedside table, he shoved those things into the pockets of the shorts—the ones he'd slept in. *Did I say something wrong?* Disappointment flooded me as my once-in-a-lifetime opportunity with Noah came crashing to an abrupt end. I wished I had more to say (preferably something sexy) but nothing came to mind. Actually, I probably should have thanked him for saving my life—because I still needed to do that—but I could only stare at him as he moved and at all the loose pieces of his blond hair, falling around his face, messed up from the night. I decided right then and there I had a thing for longer hair on a guy.

As if he knew I was still watching him, he paused to look down at me. A few moments passed, and his gaze had me practically squirming under the sheets. So much so that I forced my eyes on the wall. Unfortunately, the wall was boring and white, and my focus easily shifted back to him. Our eyes locked again and something unspoken passed between us. Whatever it was, it caused his strong jaw to clench. Then, saying nothing, he reached for the door handle and left the room.

Jesus, have mercy on my pounding heart!

I breathed out a giant huff of air—one I hadn't even realized I'd been holding in. Once upon a time, I used to be the smooth, confident one among my friends. *What the hell was that?* I'd just laid there ogling up at him like a wet blanket. Trying to shake the regret and embarrassment that was now flooding me, I sat up and crawled out of the waterbed.

Why the heck had Noah been so adamant about sleeping on the right side of the bed? It dawned on me then how that had been kind of odd. But in general, Noah himself was kind of odd, so I let the thought go. It was time to find out if Mom had called the cops when she woke up and didn't find me in my bed. I was sure I was causing her hair to prematurely go grey.

Luckily she hadn't called any authorities.

I missed Noah and Ellie leaving, but when I came upstairs Mom was there. She sat on a barstool at the island counter in the kitchen. She had her coffee and her protein shake. "Where have you been?" she asked. Usually she kept a calm air about her, but she wasn't quite as calm now. I knew she worried about me constantly these days, but I wished she wouldn't. I still wasn't sure I regretted my suicide attempt, but I wasn't about to try to do it again.

"I went for a morning walk on the beach," I answered, feeling the need to lie about my shared time with Noah.

Mom nodded. "That's good. The beach is always good for the soul." She glanced down at my pajamas. "You didn't want to change before you went out?"

Sighing, I moved for the pantry. I opened the door and hung on it, nothing inside looking very appealing. "Most of my clothes no longer fit." And *that* was the honest to God truth.

During my stay at The Cove I'd gained about fifteen pounds. My roommate, Patty, had been anorexic. That was the reason she was there. And the crazy part was, when I'd first moved in with her, I'd been the thinner one! What a wakeup call—I'd never noticed I had an eating problem. Actually, I didn't think my weight loss was necessarily an eating problem but a result of other things—like stress and depression. But on that first day, when I saw Patty's eyes take in my figure with envy, I knew I needed to make a change. If not for my own sake, then at least as an example for her.

So that very evening I'd gorged on The Cove's cafeteria food. And for the entire time I was there, I ate the way I wanted. Part of Patty's treatment meant we didn't have a mirror in our room. I hadn't realized my body had changed as much as it had until yesterday. Because when I tried on the clothes I wanted to wear home, they no longer fit. Talk about a mini panic attack—especially when I'd had to borrow some of what Patty referred to as her 'fat clothes' to wear home.

But I wasn't fat. Last night, after showering in the basement bathroom,

I'd studied my naked form in front of the mirror for the first time in four months. My body had changed…but in a good way. I no longer fit into all my size two clothing, but now I had something I'd never had before—breasts! And even if my overly-healthy, slightly diet-crazed Mom was about to tell me otherwise, I think I liked this new me.

Mom stood, heading for the microwave to reheat her coffee. "I guess we're going to have to go shopping today then. Those pajamas and the outfit you wore yesterday are hideous. You need some different clothes. And a change in wardrobe is always good."

What? I'd expected her to comment on my weight, but instead she was going to buy me new clothes. I was so relieved, I walked over and gave her a hug. And then, after shocking the heck out of her, I changed for a fun-filled day of shopping. Truthfully, I loved shopping. Almost as much as Rose loved to shop. So the three of us set out for the nearest mall…and it was a really good day.

Rose was still being very cold and strange around me, but at least her ear buds stayed out for the mall trip. When we arrived back at the house, a little after lunchtime, I debated on what to do with the rest of my day. Mom worked from home, doing most of the behind-the-scenes stuff for Dad's real-estate job. So even on Sundays both my parents were always working. Rose watched her TV shows. And that left me by my lonesome.

On a normal summer day, I might have taken a towel down to the waterfront, dug my feet into the hot sand, and worked diligently on bronzing my skin. But I wasn't ready to face the ocean head-on yet. It reminded me too much of Ben and too much of the way he'd died. I'd had lots of time to think these past four months. Ben had sacrificed his life trying to rescue someone else. After learning about my brother's death, I'd been so distraught that my immediate reaction had been to join him—wherever he might be. But with time to think…I knew he'd be disappointed in that rash decision. And so now, I was scared to death to face the ocean and step in the sand we'd spent countless hours as kids playing in.

My other option was Sonya Fletcher. My bestie. My partner in crime since kindergarten. Her father owned an all-you-can-eat crab place in Nags Head, another beach town a few miles away. I'd worked as a server at his restaurant the past two summers. Now that I was home, I assumed he'd be eager for me to start work with the rest of the summer hires. But just like Logan, I hadn't heard from Sonya once in the past four months. *Why were all my friends from high school avoiding me?* Maybe their avoidance was for the best. I felt pressure around them and having that pressure lifted while at The Cove had been pretty freaking nice.

So I settled for an afternoon nap on the living room sofa. Rose's annoying shows blared loud and made it impossible to sleep, but that didn't bother me. Ellie came by for dinner later in the evening. But much to my disappointment, Noah wasn't with her. I went to bed in my own room but once everyone was asleep, I snuck downstairs to sleep in the waterbed again.

The pillow on Noah's side still smelled of him—a mixture of soap, ocean breeze, and leather. Kind of hard to describe, but I recognized it instantly as his scent. It was nice and comforting. Too bad he wasn't around. I found myself wondering if I should have taken better advantage of him being in bed with me the night before. I thought of how his lips on my lips might feel. He might be quiet, but he had a strong, unshakeable presence about him. I wondered how those traits translated during sex. Was he secretly soft and gentle or rough and controlling?

Hot damn.

I had to roll away from Noah's side of the bed because his smell was messing with my mind. Not to mention, the blood in my veins was pumping a little too hard thinking over the possibilities.

But one thing was for certain—Golden. Opportunity. Missed.

chapter 5

NOAH

I don't know what the hell happened to me this morning. But whatever it was, it wasn't good. About a million fucking miles from good.

This morning I'd woken before Georgie. With her in bed with me, I'd been able to get my first decent night of sleep in a long time. No nightmares. No flashbacks. No constant worrying. But it was more than that, the other demons that haunted me had taken a night off too. Waking up so calm was strange, and I'd wanted the feeling to last. Therefore, I'd stayed perfectly still, listening to Georgie's soft breathing, until Ellie came pounding on the bedroom door like a maniac. Seriously, the woman needed to dial it down a notch or two.

Anyway, I'd woken and rolled out of bed—ready to chalk up my peaceful night as merely an urge satisfied. As irrational as it was, that 'big brother' protective nature I'd developed for Georgie felt at ease knowing she was safe and sound beside me. But as I'd gathered my keys and wallet off the nightstand, ready to leave, I'd stared down at a very gorgeous woman lying in the bed.

And *holy fucking shit. This wasn't what I'd signed up for.*

Brotherly affection was the furthest thing from my mind. A whole slew of other emotions came crashing down on me. Morning light streamed across her form and Georgie, curled up in bed with her silky brown hair fanned out on the pillow and her perky, braless tits straining against the fabric of her t-shirt, was the hottest fucking thing I'd ever seen in my life.

Her bright blue eyes met mine. Almost as a test, maybe just to see how she'd react, I continued staring down at her—seconds ticking by. She squirmed under my gaze but only looked away from me briefly. Then her eyes settled on me once more, confident and sure. I could tell when a woman wanted me. And Georgina Turner was looking up at me like she wanted me to rip her clothes off and fuck her until we were both so sated we couldn't move.

That sexiness she radiated…it was too much for me to handle, and I'd left the room as fast as humanly possible. And since that moment, I hadn't been able to shake her and the feeling of uneasiness that was threatening to consume me.

"What crawled up your ass, Clark?" Ellie teased, her voice bringing my thoughts back to the present. "Maybe you should pull over so I can drive."

"Huh?" I was only vaguely aware of where I was.

Driving. Oh yeah, I was driving.

"You're going twenty in a thirty-five," Ellie said. "Step on the gas, Grandpa."

The speedometer in Ellie's car came into focus, and I sped up until I reached the speed limit. I always insisted on driving when we were together because riding shotgun with Ellie was painful. The girl couldn't drive for shit. Now, it seemed, neither could I. We were late for work. Church had run later than usual. And because of my poor driving skills, Ellie and I were going to be even later for firing Patrick. It was all so ridiculous that if I hadn't still been caught up in the tantalizing images of Georgie and the way her nipples had puckered against that tattered old shirt of hers, I'd be laughing at myself right about now.

"Seriously, Noah, are you okay?" Ellie asked.

I only nodded. She'd already asked me eight times in church if I was okay. I didn't have a new answer for her. And the truth was too inappropriate to voice.

Church. Praise Jesus and all that shit. During Georgie's suicide attempt, while holding her in my arms and watching her almost die, I'd made a deal with God. *Let her live and I'll start going to church again.* My memaw, the grandma who had believed in ghosts, used to take me with her when I was younger. After Memaw had her stroke and was no longer able to care for me, I'd been passed along to the next relative who would take me. Uncle Joe. Joe hadn't believed in anything but booze and target practice on Sundays. God disappeared from my life, and I used to think 'good riddance.' But I hadn't missed a Sunday in four months now, and I didn't hate going.

Besides, it sure was fun to watch Ellie singing and dancing along to every hymn. But today was different; today I was off. Ellie had easily noticed, and I was finding it harder than hell to get back on track.

We turned into the parking lot of The Presidential Swing—a miniature golf course featuring USA themed decorations and whatnot. Lame, yes. But it was mine and therefore I was insanely proud to be called 'co-owner.' Ellie and I had taken over the place roughly three years ago, and I was honored by the way happenstance had led that to happen. I parked at the end of the parking lot and followed Ellie toward the main building—where refreshments, rounds of mini golf, and buckets of balls for the driving range were sold. Kill Devil Hills, sandwiched between the towns of Nags Head and Kitty Hawk, was part of the northernmost portion of the Outer Banks and around here miniature golf courses were like pizza places in New York City—plentiful. But business was plentiful too, and we'd managed to turn a decent profit the past three summers. I only hoped this summer would be the same.

"Hi, Patrick," Ellie said as we came inside the building and approached the counter. Three employees were currently working inside—two summer hires (Patrick and another girl about his same age) and Jill, the supervising manager.

Jill gave me a big smile and a wink. The flirtatious woman was in her early thirties with big green eyes and red hair she typically wore in a ponytail. I didn't know too much about Jill. Sure, she'd been working here about as long as I had, which was almost eight years now, but we'd never been closer than casual acquaintances. She was a hard working employee, always on time, but I liked keeping my relationship with her very surface. In fact, besides Ellie and a couple others, that was exactly how I kept all my relationships.

"Noah and I need to speak with you in the break room," Ellie said to Patrick. Her normally booming voice had softened. "Right now, please."

Patrick—about eighteen, skinny, with short, spiky hair—looked like he was about to piss himself. He didn't once even glance in my direction as he left his spot and moved toward the back of the building. *Jeez,* I thought sarcastically, *this was going to be about as fun as walking across hot coals barefoot.* The three of us squeezed ourselves into the empty break room. I left the door slightly ajar behind us.

"I'm sure you already know what this is about," Ellie said, motioning for Patrick to sit in one of the chairs. He sat and then Ellie sat in the second chair across for him. I remained standing. "I caught you stealing yesterday, and we don't tolerate that here. I'm really sorry. Seriously, I wish things could have been different because I thought you were going to be a good employee when we hired you, but we're going to have to let you go." She shrugged like she didn't give a shit when I knew she really did. "It's policy. You shouldn't have stolen."

Patrick buried his face in his hands. "I promise it will never happen again," he whimpered. "Give me one more chance. I need this job."

"I'm sorry, but you already had your chance and you blew it. There are plenty of other kids your age who'd love to have this summer job—plenty of others I won't have to worry about stealing." Ellie stood, her face stone-cold and decided. "You'll get paid through today. Take a few moments and then please leave."

Then Ellie 'the bad-*ass* cop' walked past us both, leaving me alone with Patrick.

"If you want you can reapply next summer," I told the sniffling boy. "I can't make any promises, but if you're around Kill Devils and looking for a job, we'll consider you at that time."

Shit.

I hardly knew what else to say. Ellie had already said it all. I walked out of the break room and toward the front of the store. Jill and the other girl were helping some customers. Ellie had already disappeared, but I knew my friend, and I knew where I could find her.

Cutting across the parking lot, I went straight for Ellie's car. Sure enough, she was inside—bawling her eyes out. I hadn't seen her cry this hard since Ben's death. As tough as she appeared on the outside, she was soft as hell on the inside.

Pulling open the passenger door, I joined her in the car. "You're amazing," I said. I wrapped one arm around her. "I thought I was supposed to be the bad cop. In fact, I'm a little pissed off. I was looking forward to firing the kid."

She huffed out a resemblance of a laugh.

"I'm proud of you, Ellie. You didn't need me."

"Yes, I did," she sniffled.

We sat silently for a few minutes while she finished crying.

"Why don't you take the rest of the day off?" I suggested. "It's not even busy today. You deserve a day off after that. Just come back and pick me up around close."

"I'm sorry I was giving you such a hard time this morning. You seem fine now."

"I'm not exactly fine," I said, thinking of how I'd reacted so easily to her little sister this morning. Frankly, it was fucked up, and I was still upset at myself over that.

"What? Do you want to talk about it?" Ellie asked, switching gears instantly. Now her concern was only for me.

"No, I don't. Not yet, at least." I climbed out of the car, hanging on the open door for a moment. "Get out of here," I told her. "Go get your nails done or some shit like that."

"Shut your mouth!" she barked at me, laughing, and then sped away.

* * *

The rest of the day passed uneventfully. I had to dodge a few unwanted passes from Jill, but that was typical. Ellie came back a little after eleven to pick me up. The evenings were our busiest times and despite my decent night's sleep with Georgie, I was exhausted by the end of the day.

Ellie and I lived in a modest three bedroom, two bath single family home. We'd rented here for two years now—us and our roommate Rhett. Ellie was quiet on the drive home and even more so when we arrived home. She said goodnight and disappeared into her room. I disappeared into mine, getting ready for bed.

Finally, alone for the first time all day—alone with my thoughts. I usually craved time alone and enjoyed the quiet. But all thoughts were reverting back to Georgie. *Fuck. What the hell was wrong with me?* I tossed and turned, unable to find sleep. I guess I was worrying again— worrying about Georgie and the possibility that nothing was okay with her. Dammit, would my stressing over her ever end? Not to mention, thinking in a totally different direction—I also couldn't help but wonder where the girl had ended up sleeping tonight. Was Georgie in her bed or mine?

Before I turned eighteen, before I was able to escape living under the same roof as my uncle, I'd often snuck out and spent the night at Ellie's house. The bottom level made it very easy to come and go, although I'm pretty sure Mrs. Turner was well aware that I used to spend the night at her house. So many of my nights were spent staying in the guestroom that I still had a tendency to think of it as my own. Foolish, yes, but it had been the only place I'd felt safe during that time. And thinking about Georgie snuggled under of the covers of *my* old bed was doing something funny to my brain. And to be honest, it was doing unwelcome things to other parts of my body, as well.

Holy shit.

I left my bed for a glass of water. Maybe I would dump it on my head.

The clock on the stove read two in the morning. *Hell, when did it get so late?* I started digging in the cupboard, still fucked in the brain, when my shaky hands accidently dropped a glass onto the kitchen floor. It shattered, little pieces of glass scattering all across the tile floor. The noise sounded like a gun shot against the still, dark night.

"Ah!" Ellie yelled from her room. "What was that?!"

A moment later she came stumbling out into the living room—like a zombie awakening from the dead. Rhett came out of his room next. I hadn't even realized he was home. Behind him stood a blonde. I vaguely recognized her. She was probably one of what Ellie called his 'bar bunnies'—the girls who frequented the bar his cover band played at on the weekends and more often frequented his bed.

Rhett had a baseball bat in his hand. *Was he going to beat us all to death?*

"Put down the bat, Rhett," I said, calmly. "You couldn't hit for shit even when you were on the Daredevils, and it was me who made the noise." I motioned to the shattered glass.

Bar Bunny giggled.

"What?" Rhett asked, rubbing a hand over his closely shaved head as he set the bat down. "What are you doing anyway? Other than breaking shit?"

"There was a rat," I lied. The words popped out of my mouth before I could stop them.

"And you decided to throw a glass at it?" Rhett asked, chuckling.

I shrugged. "Something like that."

"Wait, what?" Ellie asked, suddenly wide awake. "Did you just say *rat*? You've got to be fucking kidding me. First we had those weird silverfish bugs and now rats! I'm getting the hell outta here. Now!" She turned on her heel and disappeared into her room. Less than ten seconds later she returned with her wallet and keys. "I know you and your OCD can't handle disease-carrying rats—let's go, Noah. I'm too tired for this bullshit. We're going to Mom's."

"I don't have OCD," I mumbled.

"Like hell you don't. I'll be in the car. Clean up the glass because I know you need to. I'd offer to help, but you'd just criticize the way I clean." She shook her head and went for the front door. "Meet me outside when you're finished. Please, try *not* to take all night."

Rhett laughed, not caring about my 'rat' or my so-called 'OCD.' "C'mon, sugar," he said to the girl, probably unable to remember her name. "Let's go back to bed. Ellie's right; Noah is particular about cleaning so it's better to leave him alone." He pulled on the girl's arm, leading her back toward his bedroom. She bit her lip and didn't put up an ounce of fight as she disappeared with Rhett behind his door.

Taking a deep breath, I hurried to clean all the glass off the floor. First

I swept, then I vacuumed, and then I swept again. After that, I filled a backpack with a few things to take over to the Turner's, and I did it all while fighting the urge to sweep for a third time. I didn't have Obsessive Compulsive Disorder, but I did need to keep a certain level of order in my life. Ellie and Rhett liked to tease me about it, but I didn't care.

By the time Ellie and I drove the short distance over to the Turner's house, it was after three in the morning. The neighborhood streets in Kill Devil Hills didn't have big street lights, but the moon was full and bright tonight. It cast an eerie glow, and if ghosts were real, they'd be out tonight. Ellie stumbled from the car, through the door, and toward her old room in the basement. I went for the guest bedroom.

"Night, Ellie," I whispered.

She mumbled something that sounded closer to Spanish than English. Then she closed herself in her room. It took several breaths, but I turned the knob to enter the guest room. Anticipation churned in my stomach like rancid acid.

Somehow I knew Georgie would be on the other side. And where last night I knew nothing would come from sharing a bed with her, tonight I wasn't quite as certain.

chapter **6:**

GEORGINA

Caught between dreaming and consciousness, I blinked my eyes open. Someone or something had woken me. "Georgie?" A deep voice cut through the darkness and vibrated through me as I felt the intruder rest a hand on my shoulder. "Georgie, wake up."

"Noah?" I asked, rolling over. *Was I still dreaming?* "What?"

"It's late," said the voice. "I'm sorry to wake you, but can I share the bed with you again?"

I had to be dreaming, but it was a sweet-ass dream. "Okay."

"You're on my side."

Somehow I managed to end up in Noah's spot again during my sleep. Oops. But before I could move, the dark figure in my room crawled in under the covers with me. *Holy hell!* He used his body to move mine toward the middle of the bed, but he didn't roll away after he had me where he wanted me. The invisible line that had separated us last night was pretty freaking non-existent right about now. And suddenly, I was wide awake.

Oh. My. Gosh!

Noah Clark was in bed with me, and he was snuggling me! Not just snuggling. *We were fucking spooning!*

Now—obviously, I knew I wasn't dreaming because this reality was far better than a dream. His strong arms engulfed me and held my body flushed against his. The waterbed dipped slightly under our shared weight, creating a taco effect. And if he wasn't caging me in so tightly right now, I'd pinch myself because I had to be hallucinating. My poor heart—it was beating like mad inside my chest. I tried to breathe evenly, hoping Noah couldn't hear how easily he was affecting me, but I couldn't really hide it.

"Is this really happening?" I asked him between ragged breaths.

"Yes," he said, not even the least bit fazed. *Was it normal for him to crawl into bed with a random person and hug them so tightly?* I thought the guy was pretty standoffish. "Go to sleep, Georgie. I won't hurt you or touch you more than this. I slept really easily last night being near you. I want to see how well I can sleep being even closer."

Wow. I was never going to be able to fall asleep again.

"I know you would never hurt me," I whispered.

"Good."

It took almost twenty minutes in his arms before I started to relax. And when I did it happened all at once like a giant wave sweeping over me. Uncomfortableness was replaced by an easy bliss. And once I accepted it, I realized how nice being held by Noah was. There was no pressure of any kind. No expectations. No anything. Just him and me, the night, and this room. I shifted, finding a more comfortable position. I ended up with my face tucked in close against his chest.

He chuckled lightly. "Better now?"

I didn't answer. I was too comfortable to care about anything anymore. Sleep hit me hard.

* * *

My pillow shifted, waking me. It was morning, and I literally groaned out loud because of it. "No," I whined. "Don't move."

"You're making that impossible." Cracking my eyes open, I remembered that I'd cuddled with Noah last night. The plaid of his pajama pants came into focus, and I realized that I was currently using his lower stomach as a pillow, dangerously close to his...*goodies*.

I sat up super-fast.

Noah smiled at me, not even affected by the fact that I'd just had my face practically in his lap. I tried to remember if I'd ever seen him smile before. He should do it more often—he had a really nice smile.

"Sorry," I mumbled, bringing my knees to my chest.

"I'm not," he answered.

Blood rushed to my cheeks. "Did you sleep better with me?" I asked. I had to ask.

"Yeah, I did."

"Do you have sleeping problems?"

He shrugged, telling me I shouldn't push him on the subject. But I'd just had my face basically in his crotch so I think I deserved to know exactly what last night meant to him.

"Hey," I said, half-joking half-serious, "I'm the fucked-up one who tried to kill herself—a little insomnia kind of pales in comparison. So it's really okay; you can answer my question if you want to."

He sat up, moving into my personal space. His hands pushed my hair aside and gripped the sides of my face, forcing me to look him directly in the eyes. We were inches apart and my heart started racing. Despite getting to snuggle with him all night long, his touch now wasn't quite as gentle and that roughness had my full attention. "You're not fucked-up," he whispered, his voice so serious that I almost believed him. "Don't *ever* say that again. And yes, I have insomnia. Or rather, nightmares."

I swallowed hard, remembering why I'd always found him so intimidating. He could probably kill someone with his bare hands. "Well, I'm glad I helped your insomnia." I pulled out of his grip and climbed out of bed. "Maybe you should consider getting a dog. They're good at snuggling, too."

"What?" he asked confused. He didn't get it. I'd wanted last night to mean something and to him it meant nothing. I was an experiment—one that worked, but nonetheless still an experiment.

I took a deep breath, left the room, and closed the door behind me. I hurried for the stairs, trying not to feel hurt by Noah and instead bumped into Ellie. She was coming down the stairs, blocking my way up. It couldn't have been later than eight in the morning and my sister was already fully dressed for the day—in cargo shorts and a white t-shirt. "There you are. We have rats!"

"What the hell?"

"Noah and I have rats at our house," she clarified, taking a bite of the Pop-Tart in her hand. "Disgusting, right? That's why he and I had to spend the night here last night. Noah's asleep in the guestroom. I'm going to the store to get some rat poison or traps or whatever the hell I need to buy to kill those dirty little bastards. Want to come with me?"

A second later Noah came out of the guestroom. I know because I heard the click of the door, not because I turned around. I refused to turn around.

"It's a Christmas miracle," Ellie joked. "Sleeping Beauty awake before ten? I better go get my camera to mark this momentous occasion. C'mon, Georgie and I are going to the store to buy rat poison. Let's go."

"Can I go get dressed first?" Noah asked.

"If you must," my sister answered. Then she said to me, "Go get dressed, kiddo. I don't have all day. Noah and I both have to work again today since we had to fire one of our employees yesterday. Bummer, huh?"

Tentatively, I glanced back at Noah. His expression was unreadable so I looked back at Ellie. As much fun as buying rat poison sounded... "I can't go with you guys. I'm going to go see Sonya about working at her dad's restaurant this summer."

That hadn't been on my agenda for the day—nothing had, actually—but I needed something other than nothing to do. Anything had to be better than spending more time hopelessly thinking about Noah.

"Cool. Cool," Ellie said and let me pass. "See you later this evening then. Maybe if you're home early enough we can hit the beach together. Or not. We could always go get ice cream or something instead if you're more up for that than the ocean."

"Sure," I muttered, getting the distinct impression that she was well aware of my aversion to the beach. Either way, it was really nice of her to offer to hang out with me. But I hurried upstairs, because if I lingered any longer I would only give in to my impulses and stare at Noah some more.

* * *

The Fletcher family's all-you-can-eat crab place, the Blue Pelican, opened at ten thirty for lunch, but if Sonya was working she'd surely be there earlier than that. I wanted to get ready and be there to meet her before her shift started. A good number of the kids in our close circle of friends worked at the Blue Pelican too. Tips were high and since it was a buffet and people served themselves, the work was easy. I'd be stupid not to work there again this summer. Especially since it would be wise to start saving up before my first year of college—not that I was even sure what I was going to do about next year. I'd been accepted to my dream school, but the things I used to *think* were my dreams had kind of changed in the last four months.

I took a long, hot shower down in the basement after Noah and Ellie left. Then I spent a good hour and a half blow drying my hair and perfecting my makeup. I found one of my old Blue Pelican t-shirts and put that on—it was too tight over my now bigger chest, but it would have to do until they issued me a new one. I'd picked out a new pair of black shorts with Mom yesterday so I changed into those too, completing my uniform.

It was five after ten when I arrived at the Blue Pelican. They weren't open yet, but I went in through the back like all the other employees anyway. My stomach was a little uneasy since Logan Carter (my soon to be ex) worked summers here too. I wasn't exactly sure what I'd say to him when I saw him again. Maybe I'd tell him off for being such a douchebag of a boyfriend, but probably not.

I found Sonya chatting with one of the cooks. She looked exactly the same as I remembered—straight blond hair framing her delicate, heart-shaped face. Her eyes were a stunning blue color and her body...*skinny.* I used to think her figure was perfection, but now I wasn't so sure anymore.

"Hi, Sonya," I said, getting her attention. I thought it would be hard seeing her again—since she used to date Ben. I thought the sight of her would remind me too much of my brother, but I felt none of that seeing her.

"Gina," she squealed. Surprise lit up her face, telling me she definitely hadn't expected me home anytime soon. But she recovered quickly from her surprise and then gave me air kisses on both cheeks, acting all European. "What are you doing here?"

"I'm home now. I came to see you and to see if I could get my old job back."

Her blue eyes flitted over my body. "You look...*different.* What were they feeding you at that psycho place anyway?"

Psycho place? "Food," I answered.

"Well, at least your boobs are bigger," she added.

I smiled, mock feeling my chest for a quick moment. "I know. It's awesome!"

Sonya forced a small, resemblance of a laugh.

"Is Mr. Fletcher in today?" I asked, feeling uncomfortable all of sudden. This wasn't going as easy as I'd imagined. "I'd love to talk to him and see if he'll give me my old job back for the summer."

My friend stuck her hip out and leaned against the counter. Her eyes flickered to the cook for a moment, a guy I didn't know, and then they settled on me once more. "That's the thing," she said. "We've already hired all our summer help. You're out of luck."

"What?" I was dumbfounded. "Seriously?"

"Seriously."

My stomach churned. She was giving me the fucking brush off! And to make this moment worse, her eyes then glanced down at my arms. I'd worn a short sleeve shirt today, momentarily forgetting that the scars on my arms from my botched suicide attempt were still very noticeable. And she'd noticed them. Not only that, she'd made a point of noticing them in front of her cook friend and anyone else who was watching us right now.

I had to get out of there!

Mumbling a quick goodbye, I fled the restaurant as quick as possible. We'd been friends since kindergarten. *How could she suddenly treat me like I meant so little to her?* I rushed to my car. Tears threatened to pour out, but just like the other night, they never came. Come to think of it, I was not sure if I'd cried since Ben's funeral.

Getting in my car, I cranked the air conditioning and the music. Several minutes, maybe even a full hour passed. I was lost in a bunch of negative thoughts, counting each breath I took, waiting for this moment of pain to pass. All I really wanted to do was to call Patty, my roommate from The Cove. But cell phones weren't allowed, and I couldn't remember the landline number to our room. And then it occurred to me—I didn't need Sonya.

I didn't need my old life either.

High school was freaking over. Logan and I were freaking over. And I had a pretty good feeling that Sonya and I were pretty much dead too. Just like Logan, she hadn't bothered calling or visiting me even once over the past four months. *I'd almost died!* A true friend would have been there for me.

Maybe I didn't have my bestie since kindergarten anymore, but I did have someone else. Ellie. Patty had been my 'ally' at The Cove—my support system and my rock. My family had frequently visited and called, but they were too far away to be that constant I needed while I was there. I'd leaned on Patty when I'd needed her. I knew she was still only a phone call away, but in this moment I needed someone closer. I needed Ellie. And Ellie had mentioned that her mini golf place recently fired one of their employees. Maybe I could apply for a job there this summer. That sounded like a better idea than the Blue Pelican anyway.

Putting my car in drive, I headed for The Presidential Swing.

chapter **7:**

NOAH

Perfect. And now I was imagining things. I was sitting in the back office, putting the finishing touches on next week's schedule, when I swear to Christ I heard Georgie's voice. But it wasn't her voice because she wasn't here. It was merely Jill helping some customers and me losing my fucking mind.

Reaching for my bottle of water, I took a giant swig and blinked my eyes at the computer screen. I needed to focus and get my work done. It was past lunchtime, and I was starving. Only problem was the words on the computer screen kept blurring, as did my thoughts—it had been over two hours since I started what normally took me less than a half hour to finish.

Shit. The issue was…I was breaking all my damn rules. Rule Number One: No cuddling. Teddy bears were for cuddling (and dogs, apparently) and that was one big fat rule I'd thrown out the window last night. I wasn't keen on relationships—they were just messy. And if or when I was ever with a woman, I sure as hell never cuddled. And yet, breaking my rules, I'd made an exception for Georgie.

Or maybe I'd made an exception for me.

I was having trouble deciding which.

All I knew was: *fuck snuggling with a damn dog.* That sounded plain miserable and I still wasn't sure why Georgie had suggested it. If the way she'd rubbed against me and held onto me was any indication of her feelings—our enjoyment of last night had been mutual.

Seriously, fuck the damn dog.

"Noah?"

Someone called my name and I jumped a little in my seat. My arm bumped my water bottle off the desk, sending it straight into my lap. Liquid soaked the front of my pants. Son of a bitch. Now it looked like I pissed myself.

"Oh my, God! Noah, I'm so sorry," Jill gasped from the doorway. "I didn't mean to startle you."

"It's fine," I told her, patting my shorts with some computer paper. *Yep, it still looked like I pissed myself.* "Did you need something?"

"Yeah. There's a girl here who wants to apply for a job. I need an application to give her."

I stood up from my chair. Maybe I hadn't imagined Georgie's voice after all. I left the office and Jill, walking toward the front of the building. I found myself simultaneously relieved and apprehensive, while also pissed off and slightly turned on, when I spotted a stunning brunette standing with her arms crossed over her chest. Her blue eyes met mine.

Jesus, I had to catch my breath.

It was her hair. Georgie had this long, dark brown hair—straight, silky, and begging to be touched. It had been wet the first night she'd slept in my bed and in a ponytail last night, but it was down now. I'd always been partial to blondes, but I chucked that preference out the damn window, just as fast as I'd chucked out my no cuddling rule.

Or maybe it wasn't her hair. Maybe the thing about her that had me so strongly wound up was her tight little body. She currently wore a faded, worn-out t-shirt that fit snugly over her tits. I'd been thinking she'd gained a few pounds the other day and that previously she'd been too skinny. But maybe she'd always been this fucking adorable, and I'd just been the jackass who never bothered to notice.

Well, she had my full attention now. That was for damn certain.

My eyes moved back up her body and met hers once more. I'd been openly staring at her tits and instead of calling me on it or acting embarrassed, she simply smiled. "Hi Noah," she said, huffing out a little breath of air. She seemed almost *relieved* to see me.

My thoughts (and my open gawking) were interrupted by the sound of the bell on the front door chiming—followed immediately by Ellie's laughter. "Noah Clark, did you pee yourself?" She hung on the glass door, our lunch from Subway in her hand, giggling her ass off. "I swear, you're turning into the biggest klutz lately. Seriously, I need to buy a camera."

I glanced down at my pants. They were still soaked. I stepped behind the counter where the cash register was, because in all honesty, my dick was semi-hard. I'd reacted so easily to the mere sight of a *clothed* Georgina that I was sporting not only wet pants but an erection, too, both of which did not need to be Ellie's entertainment for the day. Good thing my friend was the perfect buzz-kill.

"If you buy a camera just to take embarrassing pictures of me, I will break it," I deadpanned to her.

Ellie frowned, plopping our bag of lunch down on the counter. "Relax," she told me. "It was a joke." Then she turned to face Georgie. "What's up, kiddo? How did seeing Sonya go?"

"Not as I expected," Georgie muttered, crossing her arms a little tighter over her chest. "I came to apply for a job here instead. Do you have an application I could fill out?"

"You don't have to fill out an application," Ellie answered. "You're my sister; you're automatically hired."

What?

"Thanks," Georgie said. "You have no idea—"

"Wait." Part of my brain was yelling at me to shut the hell up, which was usually what I was good at. The other part was yelling at me to do *something* about this. Georgie spending the entire summer working for me—that sounded like a horrible fucking idea. I was already moving into very dangerous territory with her. I needed to slow the hell down. "Maybe Georgie should have to fill out an application like everyone else," I suggested to Ellie. "Seems unfair otherwise."

If looks could kill then I'd be a dead man, because Ellie was gouging out my brain with her eyeballs. But still, being the complete asshole that I was, I reached into the cabinet below the counter where I knew the applications were and pulled one out. I handed the paper to Georgie. "You'll have to fill this out just like everyone else. Oh, and we check out references so please make sure you list updated phone numbers."

She nodded and took the paper from me.

Then I opened the Subway bag and grabbed (hopefully) what was my turkey sandwich. "I'm going to head over to the house and check on the rat traps," I told Ellie, moving away from the counter and toward the door. "If you decide to hire Georgie, then you can be in charge of her training and whatnot."

And with those closing words, for the first time in my life, I cut out of work early.

When I arrived home, I found that the rat traps were empty. Go figure. Ellie and I had gone to the store and bought eight of them this morning in hopes of catching my fictional rat. All eight traps were set up with different kinds of food as bait—peanut butter, cheese, raisins—in various locations around the house. At this rate, I was probably going to have to go to a pet store and buy a damn rat to release in our house. That seemed cruel though, and I hoped it wouldn't come to that.

I didn't feel bad about lying about a rodent. Ellie would probably only tease me if she knew the truth. I did, however, feel like the scum of the earth for way I'd treated Georgie this morning. With more time to think, I wondered now what had happened with her friend Sonya. Why hadn't her morning gone as 'expected?' I'd been so busy worrying about myself when I should have thought of her.

So when nine at night rolled around, and I'd cleaned our house twice—excluding Ellie and Rhett's rooms—I decided *fuck it* and headed straight over to the Turner's house. I came in through the lower level (Mrs. Turner had given me a key a few years back) and met a silent downstairs. I heard the faint sounds of people upstairs, but decided I wasn't in the mood for conversation with anyone but Georgie.

Scribbling a quick note to Ellie, apologizing and letting her know I'd be crashing here again, I popped into my friend's bedroom and left the note on her desk. I brushed my teeth in the downstairs bathroom, then crawled into the waterbed, hoping Georgie would come to sleep in this bed again.

And if she didn't come sleep down here...then I was going to go upstairs and get her myself. Last night had been unexpected and not something I was used to, but it had also been special and I wasn't ashamed to admit that.

* * *

I'd dozed off—for how long, I couldn't be certain. But I opened my eyes to a pitch-black room.

No Georgie.

I rolled over, grabbing my phone off the nightstand. The time read just after two in the morning. Hell, I guess I was going to have to make good on my threat and bring her downstairs myself. Crawling out of the warm covers, I left the guest bedroom behind. And I was just about to head upstairs when I noticed someone asleep on the tiny couch. Even in the darkness I could tell that someone was Georgie. She was curled up in a little ball with no blankets.

Fuck, I was such an asshole.

I walked across the room and had the girl cradled in my arms a second later. She woke up, mumbling something against my chest.

"It's only me," I whispered, using my backside to push open the guest bedroom door and bring her into the room with me.

I gently placed her down in the middle of the water bed and climbed in beside her. Wrapping my arms around her waist, I then pulled that sexy little body of hers against my chest. Screw boundaries. Screw the moral compass inside me that kept screaming at me that this was wrong. Screw my no cuddling rule. I wanted her close to me. I wanted to breathe in the sweet scent of her all night long. And I wanted her pretty blue eyes to be the first thing I saw when I opened mine tomorrow morning.

She didn't protest or push me away but instead nuzzled closer against me.

My fingers tingled with the need to trace up and down the curves of her body, but I fought off the feeling. Closing my eyes tight, I tried to fall back to sleep. No such luck. I was hyperaware of the girl in my arms. She seemed to be having a similar problem and kept shifting against me.

My cock twitched and strained against my pajama pants. If she was going to keep rubbing against me like this, then pretty soon I was going to act on the impulses that were begging to take control of my body.

"Georgie, sweetheart, you've got to stop moving," I whispered.

Just as I said the words, her leg accidentally brushed against my length. I was so hard I could pound nails. And now she understood *why* I needed her to stop moving. She sucked in a sharp breath and moved out of my embrace.

"Sorry," she muttered.

"I'm not. But I certainly don't want more than cuddling to happen tonight."

"Maybe I should just stay on this side of the bed then…since you don't want me like that."

Did I hear a trace of anger in her voice?

I laughed, surprised. I guess this proved it. I hadn't been mistaken that first morning. Georgie Turner *did* want me—exactly the same way I wanted her. I caught her waist and pulled back to where she belonged. My erection pushed against her hip and I let it. She needed to know how I felt. "Of course I want you like that. But I'm trying to be a gentleman."

"Maybe I don't want you to be a gentleman," she whispered, so low I almost missed it.

I kissed her shoulder—because it was the closest part of her body to my face and because I wouldn't dare kiss her mouth. Too many lines had already blurred between us.

"Not tonight," I said and let my lips linger against her skin. Then I brushed her hair away from her face and tried my best to study her through the dark. Damn, our noses were nearly touching now and I still felt like we weren't close enough. I licked my lips and pushed my length a little harder against her body.

Shit, I was losing control.

I'd never wanted to kiss someone so bad in my life. Her fingernails dug into my arms. She wanted it, too. "Please, Georgie," I choked out. "Distract me. *Now.*"

A soft moan escaped her sweet little mouth, and she only pressed her body more tightly against mine. Then, as if to torture me more, she hooked one leg high up around my hip. My hand was all over that leg—touching it and running my hand back and forth down the length of her thigh. It was a bare, smooth yet firm, and absolute heaven.

Holy shit.

"Seriously," I said, moving my hands so they instead cupped her face. "I'm gonna come in my pants if we don't stop. Tell me something. Anything. And please, stop *fucking* moving."

She chuckled and removed her leg from my hip.

Thank, Christ.

"What do you want me to tell you?" she whispered.

"Anything. Whatever." I dropped my hands away from her face—they were trembling slightly—then rolled from my side to my back. I locked my fingers behind my head so they wouldn't be tempted to touch her again. I was relieved and sort of proud of myself for being able to stop right then. Another second longer and I would have lost myself in her. "Tell me about this morning. How come you aren't going to be working at that Rusty Pelican place this summer?"

"The Blue Pelican," she corrected.

"Yeah, that's the place."

She let loose a heavy sigh and rolled onto her back. It took her a few long moments, but then she answered my question. "Honestly, I don't know. I thought Sonya and I were friends. And even though we didn't talk on the phone even once while I was away at The Cove, I never expected her to be so cold to me this morning. She said they weren't hiring at her dad's restaurant—even though her dad loves me and I'm positive that if I'd spoken with him he would have hired me. And to make it all so much worse, right before I left, Sonya purposely looked down at my arms, in front of some of the other employees there, staring at my scars like I was some kind of freak."

"Wait, what? Slow down. Who the fuck is Sonya?!" Whoever she was, I was instantly pissed at her. And at myself. I hadn't been much nicer than this Sonya person when Georgie came into my business for an application this morning. I sat up. Very. Thoroughly. Distracted. And flipped on the bedside table lamp.

"Noah," she moaned as the light blinded both our eyes.

"Who is she?" I demanded.

"Turn the light off."

"No."

She groaned and sat up also, her brown hair a wild mess around her shoulders and her blue eyes squinting angrily at me. But damn, even in the middle of the night, she was so fucking adorable.

"Who is she?" I repeated, softer this time.

"My best friend since kindergarten. I'm sure you've met her before. She always used to hang out at our house—her, me, Logan, and Ben. She and Ben used to date. But they broke up just before he joined the Coast Guard last year. I think their break-up was mutual, but I'm not sure."

Who the hell was Logan? I had no earthly clue and felt like an ass for not paying better attention before now. Thinking hard, I vaguely recalled Sonya. I'd never had a reason to care in the past so I had to rack my brain to remember her friend. "Is Sonya blond? About the same height as you?"

"That's her." She shrugged, her finger tracing absently at a spot on the bed. "The truth is, Sonya and I had been growing apart anyway. Once Ben left and our group went from four to three, nothing was the same. Senior year sucked. Sonya and I kept up appearances at school, but things were awkward between us. And I guess Ben's death and my suicide attempt destroyed whatever shred of friendship we had left."

She spoke so calmly of Ben and her ruined friendship with Sonya, but I could read what her lips weren't saying. It mattered to her. All of it did. And a small piece of the puzzle slipped into place for me. I knew there had to be more of a reason behind her suicide attempt—more than just Ben's death as the catalyst. And *this* had to be some of it.

"May I see your arms?" I asked, rather bluntly. She'd mentioned that Sonya had stared at her scars earlier today. I realized I hadn't even bothered to notice her arms at any point over the last couple days. I'd been too distracted by the rest of her body, but suddenly I needed to see them for myself. I needed to see them more than anything. "That's the reason I turned the light on," I added. I'd turned on the light to see her face, but it seemed like a good excuse now.

"Um…they're ugly."

"Please."

"It's weird that you want to see them," she muttered.

"No, it's not. Give me your arms. Please, Georgie."

It took her forever, but finally she gave in and stretched out her arms, exposing the underside of each for me. "Fine, but I'm only showing you since you've already seen them in way worse condition. And, just so you know, you're a weirdo for wanting to see them."

"I've been called worse," I replied, then took my time inspecting her arms. Each arm had a raised pink line running vertically down its length—the one on the right much longer and probably the arm she'd cut first. It was sick and twisted and fucked-up of me to think so, but I liked her scars. On the beautiful canvas that was her skin, these were her only imperfection, and I liked that. Her scars would forever connect us both to the night I saved her life. I liked that, too. I had to repress my desire to kiss each of her arms.

Instead, I reached toward the lamp and flipped the switch to turn it off. Darkness coated the room once more. "Time for bed," I whispered, lying down. I needed us both to go to sleep before I said or did anything incredibly stupid.

"Do you still want me to stay?" she asked.

Had I given her the impression that I didn't? Dammit, I was painfully bad at this—whatever this was. "Yes. Stay."

And so she stayed. Inching closer, she rested her head down on my chest. And once I felt the change in her breathing that told me she'd fallen asleep, I allowed myself to fall asleep, as well.

chapter 8:

GEORGINA

It was official. I liked Noah. A lot.

But for whatever reason, even if his body seemed to want me back, he'd made up his mind that we couldn't be anything more than cuddle buddies. He had multiple opportunities to kiss me last night and never once bothered to even attempt it, telling me without words that he didn't want to take things further than we'd already gone.

Nevertheless, the way he'd held me and spoke to me in the early hours of the morning had been…*pretty freaking awesome!* So I decided that I'd take whatever I could get from him for however long he was willing to give it. I knew my nights in his arms were limited—eventually the rat that was living in his house would be caught and his reason for staying over at my house would vanish with it.

I woke up well before the sun and before Noah. Today I decided not to linger in bed with him. The fear that my family might catch us together was overwhelming. I couldn't guess how Ellie would react if she knew—she was too unpredictable—but I knew my parents wouldn't be happy about it. Noah was older and probably way more experienced than me—not that I was inexperienced, but they didn't know that—and since I knew this thing with him was only temporary it was better to keep it our little secret.

Drawing on my inner ninja moves, I tried to carefully ease away from him. Only problem—I had zero ninja moves. The waterbed gave me away and Noah caught my waist before I could even make it one inch away. "It's not even light yet," he groaned. "Stay."

"I need to get up. I don't want to worry my mom."

He half moaned, half grunted, but his arms loosened their grip on me.

I laughed. I'd always assumed him to be the shy, loner, tormented type. I now knew that he was none of those things. Well, maybe he was still a little shy—but he certainly wasn't shy when it was just the two of us snuggled up in the dead of the night. That was for darn sure.

"Bye, Noah," I whispered, leaving him and the room before I slipped up and confessed my feelings or something equally embarrassing.

I hurried upstairs.

The last two mornings I'd lied to my mom. I'd told her I been walking on the beach as my excuse for being downstairs instead of upstairs in my bed. But today there was no need to lie since she wasn't awake yet. No one was. I considered returning to my own room. Then I briefly considered *actually* going for a walk on the beach. But I realized I still wasn't ready for that.

I moved across the room and toward the bay windows in our living room—the ones that overlooked the ocean. The view was the exact same view I'd already seen a hundred times before.

I'd tried to avoid thinking about Ben every single day since his death. But suddenly, as my eyes studied the water, the memories of my last real conversation with him came crashing down on me.

"Your brother passed all the physical exams and his aptitude test— he's committed and he's going," Mom said, shaking a wooden spoon with spaghetti sauce on it in my direction. She didn't even care that she was getting some on the carpet. "You, my dear, need to learn how to be more supportive. This is your brother's dream. Go talk to him because he leaves for Cape May tomorrow, and you'll regret it if you don't at least tell him

goodbye."

I balled my fists. "I'm not talking to that idiot! Screw being supportive. And I can't believe you and Dad aren't trying to talk him out of his 'dream.' We only learned about this so called 'dream' three weeks ago! It's all so stupid; that's what this is."

"He's eighteen. It's his decision. And I happen to think it's a very admirable career."

Mom turned on her heel and headed back toward the kitchen, telling me she was finished arguing. Meanwhile, I was so mad I could spit.

My brother and I were what my mom liked to refer to as 'Irish twins.' We weren't actual twins, but we were a mere eleven months apart and had been raised as if we were twins our whole lives. We were even in the same grade at school. We had all the same friends. He was my best friend. But we'd been at each other's throats over the last three weeks—ever since he oh-so-casually decided to drop this bomb on us all.

Ben, the older one, had secretly taken a few community college credits. And those credits had been enough for him to skip his senior year of high school and graduate early. And now the asshat was joining the Coast Guard! I guess it didn't matter anymore that he and Sonya broke up— because surely she'd have dumped his ass anyway after finding this news out.

I tried taking a few calming breaths, staring out the bay window in our family room. The sight of the ocean usually calmed me—but not right now.

And then...that was when I saw Ben. Outside. Walking along the beach.

Not thinking of anything or anyone but myself, I took off running through the house. Running outside. Running across the sand. I ran straight to where my brother was walking along the shore.

"You moron!" I screamed at him. "Why?! Seriously, why are you

doing this?"

Hearing my voice, he whipped around. We had the exact same chocolate-colored hair and blue eyes. He was my twin in every single way—except by birth—and now he was leaving me. I'd never felt so hurt in all my life. Not even that one time when Logan slipped up and cheated on me had I been in this much pain.

"It's what I want to do, Gina. Please, try to understand."

"No!" Tears streamed down my face. "One year. Why can't you just wait one more year?"

"You don't understand. High school isn't the same for me as it is for you. Every day feels like a lie—like I'm living for everyone else but me. I need to do this. And you need to understand that."

I couldn't stop crying. "What about college? I always thought we'd go together next year."

"Luke University is your dream; not mine."

What? It wasn't just my dream. It was our dream. Or at least that was what Ben had always led me to believe before today. "This isn't fair. How can you do this to me?"

"Listen to me." Ben wrapped his strong arms around me (when did he get so much bigger than me?) and held me tight. "Just because I'm running away doesn't mean I don't love you. This is what I need to do to be happy."

"So you're telling me...living at home with our family makes you unhappy?" I cried into his chest. "If you loved us, and me, then you wouldn't leave. This is a bullshit excuse for something else. And, seriously, if you go through with this and leave—then I'm going to hate you forever." Using all my strength, I pushed him away from me. Then I ran for the house.

The next morning Ben left for eight weeks of boot camp at Cape May.

And after his training, he was assigned to work on a cutter ship. I stopped paying attention to the details of where he was after that. And when he came back to visit at Christmas time, I was still angry and avoided all conversation with him. And then he died. He fucking died on me, and I was going to hate myself forever for the last mean words I'd said to him.

I'd been selfish and stupid and could never take back the way I'd treated my brother. My senior year had been the worst—nothing was right without him. And after learning he'd died on a rescue mission, trying to save some woman's life, I felt the most insurmountable pain imaginable. I couldn't erase the things I'd said to him, but I could join him. So I'd slit my wrists. Which only backfired in my face, embarrassingly enough, and now I had to live with that mistake, too.

An itchy sensation spread up my neck and all those same horrible feelings threatened to take hold of me again. My counselor at The Cove told me this might happen and now it was happening. And that scared the shit out of me. But, at least, now I knew how to better handle this sort of thing. Before The Cove I'd been pretty clueless. I only hoped I was slightly *less* clueless now.

"Hey," Ellie said, disrupting my thoughts. Without even hearing her sneak up on me, she was suddenly standing next to me. And the sun had risen. *When the hell had that happened?* "You okay?" she asked.

"I was about to go for a run."

I'd been on the track team in high school. I hadn't been on the team this year, since I hadn't been in attendance the last four months of my senior year, but I suddenly had the overwhelming urge to run. Not only that, if I ever faced a 'trigger,' then I was supposed to carry out my safety plan—a list of steps my counselor at The Cove had helped me create. Step number one was to notice if a trigger was happening—to notice the warning signs. I was noticing them now. Step two was to take my mind off my trigger. And, for me, that meant going for a run. I left Ellie and rushed toward my room for my running shoes.

I needed leave the house…*now*!

A minute later I was skipping down the steps with my tennis shoes on—ready to run. My sister was fast though and waiting just outside the front door. She had on her running shoes, as well. And to my absolute horror, Noah was out of bed and standing with her.

"What are you two doing?" I asked, avoiding eye contact with Noah.

"Going for a run with you," Ellie said, "Duh. What does it look like we're doing? Baking cookies?"

I groaned and took off sprinting—fast. I had to get away.

I bolted through the neighborhood streets, my feet pounding hard against pavement. I moved at top speed for as long as my body would allow. The fifteen extra pounds I'd gained felt like one hundred. Within minutes my stomach cramped and my hands began to shake, but I pushed myself and kept running like crazy—running away from all the regret. But I couldn't keep up this level of speed forever. Soon I slowed and collapsed. I dropped flat on my back, lying on some random person's 'more-sand-than-grass' front lawn.

Noah, of course, plopped down on the ground beside me two seconds later. I guess he'd chased me down the street. He really was a weirdo.

"Shit," he breathed, his gaze on the clouds above us. "You're fast. I could barely catch you. I must be doing something wrong at the gym."

I started to laugh, and I was not sure why, because Noah's comment wasn't *that* funny. But for some random reason I was laughing so hysterically that my stomach hurt and I was near tears. And then suddenly I *was* crying. *Seriously!? I'd been unable to cry for months and now the waterworks decide to show?* Noah was the last person I wanted to show emotion in front of. But these tears weren't the kind I could brush off with a 'there's something in my eye' kind of lie and so I had to let him witness it all.

Sitting up and dropping my head between my knees, I continued to sob. I thought of Ben, of how unfair his death had been, and of how much I wished things could be different. I let the pain wash over me because it seemed like a safe moment to do so. It was excruciating, and I had to count each breath I inhaled to manage through it, but I didn't feel the urge to kill myself like I had after Ben's funeral. Did that mean my safety plan was working? Or did it mean that maybe, just maybe, I was already stronger than I realized?

Noah said nothing; he was just there. He sat unwavering by my side as I cried. And then after a couple minutes, something happened. I was able to catch my breath and regain some of my composure. The moment I did, Noah wrapped his arms around my shoulders and pulled me in against his chest. I let him do it, too. I found I really wanted and needed a hug from him.

And then suddenly I realized—*holy smokes!*—Noah wasn't wearing a freaking shirt. I guess he must have taken it off before our run and I never noticed. His chest was slightly damp and taut and warm. It gave me a whole new idea. If he wanted to use me as his snuggle-buddy to make his nightmares go away, then I wanted to use him back in a similar way.

"Kiss me," I demanded.

"What?" He pulled away slightly. His whiskey-colored eyes stared at me full of confusion. But maybe there was a little bit of lust there, too.

"You heard me," I whispered, feeling unexpectedly bold. Noah made me feel that way. "Kiss me. Kiss me and make me forget everything bad."

He swallowed hard and started breathing a lot heavier than he was moments ago. "No," he said and stood to his feet.

What the hell! Seriously? The guy chased me down the street, stayed with me while I cried, and then held me tightly against his bare chest like I was already his. Not to mention—one hell of an erection he had in bed with me last night! But he wouldn't kiss me?

Ellie appeared about fifty yards down the street. She jogged leisurely in our direction. "Hey, guys!" she yelled, waving. "Sorry, I'm slow!"

Standing to my feet, I dusted sand off my hands and then rubbed the tears from my cheeks. I was beyond pissed. "You're a jackass," I told Noah, jogging past him and in Ellie's direction. "Seriously," I said over my shoulder. "I don't understand all your crazy mixed signals."

Noah stood and began jogging after me.

I rolled my eyes and kept running. But so did Noah. He jogged until he caught up with my stride.

"Leave me the hell alone," I snapped in a whisper at him.

"Fuck, no," he whispered back at me. "I'm not leaving you alone."

"Hey, you two," Ellie said as we met back up with her. For Noah's sake, it was good thing she was around because I really wanted to slug him in the face. Suddenly all three of us were running together. Well…I was running toward the house, and they both just happened to be moving in the same direction I was.

We jogged in silence after that. And after about five minutes, when I still wanted to throttle Noah, I decided that there was a good possibility that he might be toying with me. I realized I knew very little about the man I'd been snuggling up with the last couple nights. What if he was some psycho who got off on screwing with other people's emotions? But Ellie trusted him, so I had to rule that theory out.

Or maybe the more probable reason he'd rejected me was that he didn't like me as much as I liked him. Ouch. A sting shot through me because that *had to be* the reason. The house came back into view, and I'd never been so grateful to see it. Noah might be a jerkoff or he might not be—but either way he had a tempting-as-hell, muscular body. One that I did not need to see in motion ever again. I had to get away from him as fast as possible.

"Thanks for running with me guys," I mumbled, splitting away from them toward our house.

"I actually think I want to run a little further," Ellie suggested.

"Me too," I heard Noah reply to her. Whatever. They could run all day long for all I cared. I wasn't going with. I was going inside, and I was already halfway there. *Nearly home. Five more feet.*

"Let me talk to Georgie for a moment first," Noah said next. "Give me two seconds."

WTF?

I caught my breath and stopped running—the front door inches away. I stared at the metal door knob, listening to the sound of his shoes on the sidewalk as he approached me from behind. Maybe if I stared at the door hard enough I could melt into it.

"You don't have to say anything to me," I whispered when I felt him standing behind me. *God, what must Ellie be thinking watching us from the street?* "It's obvious you don't like me as more than a friend. I was being stupid and childish before. I'm beyond embarrassed here, so can we forget I ever asked you to kiss me?"

"Fuck, no," he replied. "Turn around, please."

What?

I turned around; I couldn't stop myself.

"Look at me."

Once again, my body reacted to his command. Our eyes connected.

Then he brought his hands to my face, cupping the sides of my jaw—effectively killing any anger I had left toward him.

"It wasn't stupid or childish," he said gently. "But when I kiss you for the first time it won't be because you were crying. And it won't be because you've asked me to. It will be because I can't go another minute without knowing what those sweet, plump lips of yours taste like. That's all. Don't hate me for needing to wait, pretty girl. I'm already in more pain than you realize."

"Noah," Ellie whined from somewhere down the street. "Are you coming or not?"

Paying her zero attention, he smiled at me and inched his body a little closer toward mine. "Is it wrong that I like you a little embarrassed and pissed off at me?" One of his thumbs traced across my cheek. "You have a hell of a lot of passion inside you, Georgie. You're fierce and a little reckless. Let those sides show more often. Maybe holding everything in is part of the reason you feel so much pain."

My heart boomed against my ribcage. I had no answer for Noah; my whole body was frozen. *Was he right about holding everything in?* I continued gazing up at him, lost in the way his eyes stared at my mouth, like we were moments away from kissing.

His hands left my face, skimmed down my arms, and took up a new home resting lightly on the sides of my waist. His voice went crazy low and he said, "I'm tempted to push you against the fucking door and do a whole lot more than kiss you right now."

My heart slammed inside my chest. But instead of carrying out his threats, he dropped his hands and stepped backward—suddenly and completely.

"I know you start work today. It's my day off so I won't see you until later." He cleared his throat. "I'm looking forward to later."

With those closing words, he jogged off toward Ellie. I turned and headed into the house, trying to act casual. But there was no freaking way I could even attempt casual. Noah hadn't kissed me, but he'd still managed to make me forget everything in the world but him. But more importantly, even if Noah hadn't been there for me just now, I still knew that I would have been fine just the same. It was an empowering feeling. One I hadn't felt in a long time.

chapter **9:**

NOAH

Ellie was going to castrate me—rip my balls off, hold me down, and spoon feed them to me. If there ever was someone I couldn't or shouldn't date—or fuck, same difference—it was her little sister. And as I slowly jogged in Ellie's direction, to where she stood waiting by the Turner's mailbox, I could already hear the earful I had coming my way. I knew what she would say because it was the exact same stuff I'd been thinking to myself all morning.

I was twenty-four. Georgie was only eighteen. I craved stability in my life. She possibly was the very definition of unstable. I had a career and my future already plotted out. I didn't know if Georgie would go to college at the end of the summer or stay here or join the damn circus. All I really knew was that the girl was a wild card. And I had a strict 'no wild cards policy.'

But in that moment, and in all my moments with Georgie, I didn't care.

"What was that about?" Ellie asked as I approached.

I shrugged. "I had to make sure she was okay."

"Is she okay?"

"I think so. I hope so."

"You know," Ellie said, her eyes narrowing at me. *Uh oh, here it comes.* "I'm not an idiot."

"Okay," I replied.

I knew she wasn't an idiot. Ellie and I had both been excellent students in high school. Two nerds, really. But after graduation, when I decided I didn't want the debt from all the student loans it would have taken to put me through college, she decided to stay behind with me. I'd tried my damnedest to convince her not to, but she'd been her typical stubborn self. She'd told me, *why waste all that money on a piece of paper when I'm happy here in Kill Devil Hills with you.* I guess, in retrospect, we'd both made a good choice. Six years later and we were both successful business owners. But truthfully, I couldn't have done it without Ellie. She was much smarter than she liked to let on so I knew I could no longer bullshit her.

"You made up the rat story, didn't you?" she asked.

What? My jaw kind of dropped. "Am I that bad of a liar?"

She shook her head. "No, but you're so in love with your Dyson vacuum cleaner that you probably jack off to the damn thing before bed every night. Which is fine, whatever floats your boat, but don't try to tell me we have rats when you're the biggest neat-freak son of a bitch I know. No rat is going to want to make a home at our place. It's too clean! Anyway, if you wanted to keep spending the night at my parents' house to be closer to Georgie you should have just asked." Ellie huffed out a great big sigh and then took off running. "C'mon, drama queen, let's run."

"Wait." I hurried after her, catching her pace in a few short strides. "You're not going to tell me to stay away from her?"

"No, I'm not. You're a big boy. She's a big girl. Do whatever you want."

"But she's your little sister. I knew her when she was only ten."

"So. She's not ten anymore."

No. She certainly fucking wasn't.

For about the millionth time in my life, I was in awe of Ellie. Her big heart had a way of continuously surprising me. I shouldn't have expected her to be anything but accepting. "You're the coolest person, you know that right?"

"Save the sappy shit for my sister."

I laughed. "Maybe I will."

"But know that if you ever hurt her, then I will hurt you."

I almost opened my mouth to say, *I would never hurt her.* But the truth was—relationships never ended well with me. And it was *me* who was the problem. I broke hearts. No matter how hard I always tried not to, it *always* happened that way. I couldn't let Georgie become another one of my casualties.

Jesus Christ.

Feeling almost comforted that I hadn't given in and kissed her earlier, I decided that my small obsession with the girl and her wellbeing was becoming borderline unhealthy. I needed to quit her cold turkey. Tomorrow.

Tonight will be your last night sharing a bed with her, I assured myself. *And then you'll have to end things with her. Cleanly and gently.* And even if my whole body ached because I hated that decision, I was going to have to follow through with it. Because I would do *anything* to protect Georgie—even if that meant protecting her from myself.

* * *

It was my day off so I did the usual—morning at the gym, the grocery shopping, followed by lunch at Chancy's Claw. The place was right on the water, indoor and deck seating, with a very 'beachy' atmosphere. As cliché as it was, it was my favorite bar in the whole Outer Banks. Rhett and his cover band played a gig there about once a week. They weren't half-bad, but Rhett also had to work as a bartender at Chancy's to make a living. Whether he was working or not, the place was his second home, and I knew I'd find him there.

I needed some company and a distraction.

And sure enough, Rhett was there. He sat perched on his usual barstool—the one toward the back of the restaurant. And he had...*his head resting on the bar top? Was he drunk at noon in the middle of the week?* Not his usual.

"Hey," I said cautiously. He was an emotional drunk. The worst kind.

"I'm glad you're here," he replied, coming alive at the sight of me and maybe not as drunk as I'd initial thought. "I need your advice."

"Okay?" Sitting down in the seat beside him, I nodded at Luce, the bartender currently working. She knew me, and she knew what I liked to order. She grabbed a pint glass and started filling it with one of Chancy's craft beers.

"What's going on?" I asked Rhett.

"I'm in mother*fucking* love."

Okay then. Not what I ever expected from him.

Luce, overhearing Rhett and obviously shocked by his words, dropped my full glass of beer onto the bar top. It spilled everywhere, including on my shorts. *Great. Fantastic. Where was Ellie with her camera?* My shorts were soaked and for the second time this week it looked as if I pissed myself. Luce apologized, brought me some napkins, and then a replacement beer. At least the napkins worked better than computer paper, but I still had wet shorts. Whatever. "What were you saying about love?" I asked Rhett instead of dwelling on my uncomfortable situation.

"The blonde. The one who stayed over the night you chucked one of our glasses at the rat. I'm in love with her, but I don't even know her name or how to find her. She used me for sex. Mercifully. And now she's gone."

He wasn't making any sense. The girl he'd had over that night...she'd looked familiar to me. "I thought the blonde was one of your bar bunnies."

"My what?"

Lowing my voice, because Luce was also one of his bar bunnies, I whispered, "It's what Ellie calls the girls you screw around with regularly. You know, like Luce and Chelsea...and maybe that brunette named Allie, too. I don't know how many of them you fuck."

"No." He sipped at the bottle of Bud he'd been palming since I walked into Chancy's. "She was different. She was more than sex. I spent the entire day yesterday going to every business from Nags Head all the way up to Duck searching for this girl. Nothing. I met her here first. So after yesterday's mad search, I decided that I'd probably have better luck staying in one place. I'm not moving from this seat until they kick me out."

That was a bit crazy, but I liked it. "What advice did you need from me?"

He shrugged. "I don't know. You've always got your shit in control. I need some of that to rub off on me right now because I feel like I'm spiraling out of control. I'm trying to ignore the possibility that I might never see this girl again." He tipped his beer back and guzzled the remainder of his drink.

I finished my beer as well.

Rhett knew very little of my past. Ellie knew more than most because she was nosy, but I still had my secrets and I worked hard at maintaining the control I had in my life. So it was a damn good thing I'd already decided to end things with Georgie. Tomorrow. And I told myself, even if it felt a little like a lie, that I never wanted to find myself in Rhett's position.

"Let's play a game," I suggested, nodding at Luce for another beer. "Every time a girl walks in the front door and she isn't *your* girl then we take a drink. Sound fun? We'll see how drunk we can get before she shows."

That got a chuckle out of Rhett. "Game on, Noah."

* * *

My pulse was pounding in my ears and it felt like someone had hit me over the head with a sledge hammer. One beer with Rhett had turned into...*damn*, I couldn't remember how many it had turned into. I'd lost count and track of time. But I was in bed now. Soon Georgie would be here with me and that was all that mattered. I wondered how long I'd have to wait before she snuck downstairs and crawled in under the covers. She *would* come to me tonight, right?

She'd better or I would go find her.

Images of her flushed cheeks and tear-filled eyes flooded my mind. I should have kissed her when she asked. I should have kissed those tears away for her. Why had I been so stubborn? She'd been hurting and seeing her hurt was the worst fucking feeling on the planet. I wouldn't let it happen again.

Wait. *Why was I in my own bed?* Not my bed at the Turners, but my actual bed at my actual house. Not to mention, it was still really light outside. That was weird.

Standing up, the blood rushing to my head, I stumbled out of my room. I guess Rhett and I drank a little too much. Where was Rhett? My memories were foggy and I had a gap in time. And then I saw Ellie standing in the kitchen—one of her damn cherry Pop-Tarts in her hand.

Fuck. It was tomorrow.

"What time is it?" I demanded.

She glared at me like I just told her to go screw herself. "Don't take your hangover out on me," she snapped. "I'm the one who picked your drunk ass up last night. You're welcome."

"Thanks," I mumbled. "But why did you bring me here?"

"Where else did you want me to bring you? Disney World?"

Groaning, I turned and rushed for the bathroom. Up until this very moment I'd been unsure of what Georgie meant to me. Sure, she was fucking gorgeous and I felt strangely protective over her. But I'd been resisting her—resisting because everything inside me screamed that something real with her could never work. I'd get hurt. Or worse, she'd get hurt.

But like it or not, something profound had happened to me when I found her on that bathroom floor, moments away from death. I still wasn't sure what that something was or why it meant I couldn't get her out of my head. All I knew was that I hadn't been there for her last night. I hadn't held her in my arms. I hadn't woken this morning to her bright blue eyes. And that wasn't okay. It was about a million fucking miles from okay. And the sinking feeling that formed in my stomach because of my lapse in judgment—it was pretty damn unbearable.

I stripped and jumped in the shower, hurrying through the motions of cleaning myself. I brushed my teeth, dressed, and then went for the garage—my Ducati was parked there and it was much faster than my car. I had to work today and was already two hours late. It was Ellie's day off. I also knew—since I made the schedule and figured Ellie would have given Georgie all Patrick's old hours—that she should be working today. I was a jackass, but I hoped like hell that she hadn't quit on account of my stupidity.

Revving my motorcycle's engine, I sped off toward work. It was only a few short miles away, but…*shit*, I had butterflies the entire ride. And no, it wasn't from the wind in my hair. Butterflies weren't something a real man should ever admit to, but I couldn't deny the fluttery anxious-nervous feeling I had going on in my stomach. That sensation poked and scratched my insides like I'd swallowed a bunch of pine cones. It was a mixture of self-loathing and excitement over the fact that I was about to see her while

I now knew exactly what I wanted.

Her. I wanted her.

Screw ending things. From the way my stomach was aching, I knew that wasn't the solution. I reached the parking lot, found a spot, but couldn't bring myself to walk inside. *Jesus Christ! Stop being such a pussy, Noah,* I told myself. *She's just a girl. A beautiful girl, but still only a girl.*

I pulled my phone from my pocket, deciding that maybe I'd call before charging inside. I was worked up, oddly excited, and the 'raging bull' approach suddenly seemed like the wrong one. I didn't want to fuck this up any more than I already had.

Dialing The Swing's main phone line, my cell rang and rang. I could see the front doors from where I stood—people going in and out—and so I figured my phone call was being ignored since they seemed busy. Finally, someone answered. That someone was Georgie. *Thank, Christ.*

"Thank you for calling The Pres—"

"Georgie," I said, cutting her off. "It's Noah."

"Oh. Hi." Her voice went soft, barely audible over the child I could hear screaming in the background. "Aren't you supposed to be here right now?"

"Yes. I'll be there soon."

"Did you need to talk to someone else?" she asked. That damn child was still screaming in the background. *And hell no I didn't want to speak to anyone else.*

"No. I called because I wanted to speak with you. Only you."

Then the line went dead.

What? Dammit.

She'd hung up on me. Not that I didn't deserve it. I took a deep breath, realizing exactly what I needed to do next to make this right, and walked across the parking lot toward the main building. I pushed open the glass doors and entered.

And there she was—behind the counter, the phone still in her hand, helping a customer at the cash register. She had a fraction of a smile on her face, one being directed at the woman she was helping, but it quickly faded as her eyes looked up and found me.

"Georgina," I said. I didn't mean for it to, but my voice boomed. "I need to see you in my office. Now." Without waiting for a response from her or any of the people in the room, I turned and headed for my office. I left the door open behind me as I disappeared inside.

chapter **10:**

GEORGINA

I wanted to slap my manager, Connie. Noah had called, and he'd called wanting to speak with me. He'd actually sounded kind of sweet on the phone which had been surprising since he never came over last night. All night and all morning I'd been assuming he hadn't shown because there was another girl, perhaps even a girlfriend since I didn't know otherwise. Maybe he'd blown me off for her. Or maybe he simply hadn't wanted to deal with my craziness. I had, after all, randomly cried on some person's lawn in front of him yesterday.

But then he'd called and restored a fraction of my hope. But my hope was quickly squashed by Connie's manicured little finger. She'd pressed the button to end my phone call! Without even a warning! While I was still using it!

"We're too busy for personal phone calls. Save it for later, honey," she'd said. How had she even known it was personal? Maybe because my cheeks were hotter than the sidewalk in July?

Connie had been fairly nice all morning (nicer than Jill yesterday) and so her behavior had come as a major shock. I guess she was under a lot of stress since there was currently a birthday party of twenty-five girls crammed into the main building, all trying to pick out a different colored ball for miniature golf.

Then Noah walked in—not two minutes after I'd hung up on him. I was still frozen with the phone in my hand. But suddenly he was here and in the same room as me. "Georgina. I need to see you in my office. Now," he'd announced to the entire room, his voice silencing everyone. He might have sounded vaguely sweet on the phone, but now he only sounded pissed off.

Then he—with his blond hair down, slightly wet as if he'd only just showered, and carrying a motorcycle helmet under one arm—stormed into his office. He left the door open behind him, obviously meaning for me to follow.

Oh. My. Gosh. He was going to fire me. Apparently Carrie thought so too because she gave me a look that seemed to say, *what did you do?* And much to my increased horror, Noah happened to look extra gorgeous today—in a ruggedly handsome, bad-boy, rip-your-clothes-off, maybe-he-really-should-join-a-motorcycle-gang sort of way.

What a way to add insult to injury. He hadn't shown up last night and now he was going to fire me. I left the woman I was helping, because what other choice did I have, and followed in the direction he'd disappeared. I hadn't seen his office yet, but I guess I was going to see it now.

Entering the room, I found it was nicer than expected. Small but tidy. *But who cared about what the freaking room looked like when Noah was in it!* He stood, leaning against the single wooden desk that occupied the space. His arms were crossed tightly over his chest. He had on a white t-shirt, jeans, and a black leather jacket.

Oh good Jesus, the guy shouldn't be allowed to wear leather. It just wasn't fair to the rest of the world.

And, of course, now my hands were trembling. I'd never been so nervous in my entire life.

"Close the door," he said softly.

I closed the door but didn't dare venture further than a single step into the room. I was finding it very hard to breathe…and to stand. "So I didn't mean to hang up on you," I blurted out. "That was an accident."

"Good to know," he said, not moving but staring pretty intensely at me. "How's your second day going?"

"Fine. I guess."

"Don't let Connie stress you out. She gets rattled when it gets busy."

I nodded. Was this what he called me in here to talk about? At least, I guess, he wasn't going to fire me.

"About last night—" he started. *Oh holy shit, we weren't just going to talk about work stuff!* And out of fear of what might come next, my lungs felt like they'd caught on fire. And my cheeks started suffering from a similar problem. "I wasn't there."

I swallowed, hard. "I noticed."

"And I'm sorry for that."

He was?

He stood up from where he was leaning against the desk. And, as if he suddenly remembered he was wearing a jacket in the middle of June, he took it off and flopped it down on his desk. Then he took a step in my direction, his gaze flickering down to my lips. Then his eyes returned to mine, staring so fiercely at me that I took a step backward. My ass hit the door behind me.

"I was thinking," I blurted out, stopping him before he could come any closer. "Um. Maybe we should just be friends. Maybe that would be easier."

Did I actually want to be 'just friends?' *Hell to the no!* But I had to let him off the hook. I had to give him an out. We'd snuggled in bed now— twice. (Three times if I were to count the first night.) And I wanted a whole hell of a lot more from Noah than that, but he'd been giving off the vibe that he didn't want the same thing. And if he couldn't give me what I wanted—everything, I wanted everything—then what was the point of starting something at all? He'd gotten my hopes up yesterday and when he never showed last night, I'd admittedly been a little crushed.

"Friends?" he asked, his eyes narrowing. "I don't have any girls that are friends."

"Ellie's your friend."

He took a step closer and then another. "Ellie's like one of the guys. She doesn't count."

"So you don't want to be my friend then?"

The idea of that hurt like hell.

"No fucking way," he answered.

At the same moment those horrific words slipped of his mouth, one of his hands touched my stomach. It was a gentle touch but bold and totally unexpected. I looked down, so surprised he had touched me that my eyes needed to see what was happening in order to believe it. I watched as his fingers trailed along the hem of my shirt and then disappeared under the material.

His fingers made contact with my bare skin. And I couldn't help it when I sucked in a sharp breath because of it. As light as a feather, his touch moved over my navel and across my stomach, shivers shooting up my spin, until his hand reached the small of my waist.

"Look at me, Georgie, please," he whispered.

I lifted my gaze to meet his. His whiskey-colored eyes were the most beautiful things imaginable. Maybe they reminded me of whiskey, not because of the color, but because of the way they warmed me deep inside.

He rested his other hand on the door beside my head.

"I want to be more than a friend to you," he murmured. His head dropped to my shoulder and his lips found my neck. "Much more. And that scares the shit out of me. I'm not very good at *more*. But for you...I think I could be damn good at it. Would it be easier to only be friends? Fuck no. I woke up this morning feeling like shit. And not because I was slightly hung-over, but because you weren't in bed with me."

"Really?"

"Yes, really."

Did that mean I wasn't just a snuggle-buddy to him?

Answering my unspoken question, he started planting little kisses along my neck where his lips touched. The stubble on his face brushed across my skin. It felt amazing, way too insanely amazing, and I gave in to his touch instantly. I tilted my head to the side to give his lips better access. My body was tingling *everywhere*. I felt high and giddy and buzzing with life. I could barely believe this was happening. Like it was too good to be true or something. But I didn't want to overanalyze the moment; I only needed him to kiss me. Now.

"Noah," I whispered. "Please."

"Tell me what you want."

I couldn't actually ask him to kiss me—not after the way he rejected me yesterday. "More," I said instead. "I want more too."

"Good," he half-growled. And then he lifted me up in his arms. It happened so suddenly that I let out a little whimper. He carried me away from the door and to the desk. Pushing his jacket and laptop to the other side, he set me down. My butt was on the hard wood and my knees pressed into his stomach. He inched my thighs apart and settled between the space he'd created.

My hands came to rest on his biceps. They were strong, hard, and quite intimidating. But that roughness Noah exuded—well, it could turn incredibly gentle at a moment's notice. Slowly and carefully, he brought his hands up the sides of my neck, digging his fingertips into my hair, ensuring that the only place I could look was right into his eyes.

He lowered his face closer to mine.

Then the door to Noah's office burst wide open.

I screamed. I literally screamed while Noah groaned.

It was Ellie, and she wasn't even surprised when she caught us together. "Oh. Hi guys. I brought you lunch." She set a grocery bag down on the desk beside us. "You know that Connie is out there basically pulling her hair out, right? She's extra stressed today. Maybe she's on her period. Want me to cover the front with her for a half-hour while you two eat?"

Noah stepped away from me while I awkwardly slid down from the desk. "That was nice of you to bring us food," I said, trying to act casual but still in total shock that Ellie didn't care about me almost kissing her best friend.

Ellie shrugged. "I was bored."

"She wasn't bored," Noah said to both of us and to neither of us. He walked toward the door. "She was being nosy, like usual, and wanted to see for herself what was going on between us." He sighed, brushing his fingers through his hair. His eyes flickered briefly to mine and then to the door. "I don't feel like eating. Rain check?"

I nodded, confused. *Was he ready to leave me so fast?*

"I'll go out front with Connie for the time being. You guys eat. Do some sister bonding or whatever."

He was about to walk out the door but abruptly stopped. It was like he suddenly realized that he was being rude—about to leave me high and dry after almost kissing me two seconds ago.

He crossed the room to where I still stood awkward and waiting by his desk. He cupped my face in his hands and swiftly gave me the kiss he hadn't moments ago. As far as kisses go, it was exceptionally tame. Just a quick press of his warm, soft lips to mine. But it was also sweet as hell, unexpected, and reassuring. It was as if he wanted me to know, in his own particular Noah way, that he hadn't forgotten about me.

He said nothing more, but I could see the hint of a smile on his lips. Then he left the room.

"Oh. My. Word," Ellie said as soon as he disappeared. "I've never seen Noah like this."

Stuck in a bit of a 'Noah daze,' my mind still attempting to process the last few moments and my heart beating out of control, I peeled my eyes off the door and refocused my attention on Ellie. "What do you mean?"

She shrugged, digging through the random snacks in the grocery bag she'd brought. "Normally he's the poster boy for cool, calm, and collected. He always has his shit together, even when I don't, but the last few days he's been...*different*. You've got him flustered and acting like a total fool. It's cute."

He didn't seem flustered to me. He seemed perfectly in control. "Are you sure?"

"Trust me. He's in deep, kiddo, and it's *really* entertaining for me to watch. I'm going to go buy a camera as soon I leave here. I can't *not* document this with at least twenty-four megapixels."

I laughed and grabbed a Lunchables from Ellie's bag. "I think you're imagining things," I said but secretly hoped she wasn't. I wanted Noah to be 'in deep,' even if the thought was only a fantasy, because the truth was, I was already in pretty damn deep myself.

* * *

Lunch with Ellie was nice. Casual. Easy. She told me all about her softball team. Yep, my lesbian sister was on a recreational softball team. Cliché but true. Apparently Noah and Rhett—who I learned was their third roommate—were on the team, too. And she wanted me to join, but I felt hesitant. Whatever I had with Noah was too new, likely only going to be temporary, and I didn't want to take over his life any more than I already had. So I declined Ellie's offer. It was a thoughtful offer though, and I promised to go to some of her games this summer.

A quick half hour later, we finished eating lunch. Ellie gave me a hug goodbye and set off to buy a camera, while I rejoined Connie and Noah. I was nervous as holy hell, still caught up in my tame-but-wonderful-still-can't-believe-it-actually-happened kiss with Noah.

"You should go on your lunch break now," Noah said to Connie the very moment I left his office. "Take an hour if you'd like. I know it's been a weird morning, but I'd really like you to start your time now since I'm already behind on everything I need to do."

"Alright," Connie responded. She shot me a look from behind the cash register. I wondered if she thought I was getting special treatment by getting to take my impromptu break before her. Whatever. I was still kind of annoyed with her for cutting off my phone call earlier so I didn't care if I'd received special treatment or not.

Ellie told me yesterday that typically only two (and on occasion three) people worked the front counter at a time. Actually, one person could probably manage the work alone—there wasn't much to do other than ring customers up at the register, answer the phone, and from time to time help little kids pick out a putter—but she said she preferred two people to always be working. I guess Noah couldn't leave me alone until Connie returned. That meant I had one solid hour of semi-alone time with Noah.

Lord have mercy on my pounding heart!

Connie left, walking off toward the break room, and I replaced her spot—as calmly as possible—behind the cash register. The only other people in the room were a teenage couple, probably not much younger than me, picking out balls for the course. They decided on pink and blue and then disappeared out the door.

"I'm assuming Ellie or Jill already showed you how to do everything yesterday," Noah said, leaning against the opposite end of the counter. Only three feet separated us.

"Yeah, I think so."

"And you're probably already a pro at it so I'll just stay over here and enjoy my view."

And he wasn't even kidding. He stayed in the same spot, with his arms crossed, and made a big show out of diligently watching me work. He didn't help me once during our time together, the bastard. Except when the phone rang and he dove for it saying, "Better let me. You might hang up on whoever's calling."

I wanted to smack him over the back of his handsome head—but changed my mind because that was when I realized that Noah was *flirting* with me. I'd never thought of him as anything but the embodiment of the strong, silent type. So seeing this other side of him came as a bit of shock and right now he was being downright playful.

"We close at eleven tonight," he told the person on the phone, while his eyes continued to stare at me, a small cocky smile working its way over his lips. "Okay. Thanks. Bye." He hung up the phone and returned to his arms-crossed-face-stern-watch-me-like-a-hawk-because-this-is-how-I-flirt routine. I liked it. He was acting panty-dropping cute, and it made me desperately want to find out what playful Noah was like in bed—with zero inhibitions holding him back.

Way too soon, disappointingly enough, Connie reemerged from the break room. Had an hour passed so fast? Bummer. "I'm finished," she told him. "I hope you don't mind, but I only felt like taking a half-hour break."

That bitch.

"No problem." Noah glanced down at his watch and then at me. "What time do you get off? Two, right?"

"Yes."

He nodded, leaving the spot he'd been glued to for the last half hour. "Okay good. Don't leave without finding me first," he muttered as he passed me.

That meant I was left alone with Connie all over again. Big dramatic eye roll.

"What did you do to piss Noah off?" she asked after he'd disappeared. I swear to the man upstairs, prior to her break she'd had on a normal amount of makeup, but now she had on twice as much. I sure hoped that wasn't for my benefit because the only thing on my mind right now was an image of Noah Clark and the way he looked in his leather jacket. It was a very good image, too, and I had a feeling I was going to need to focus on that image in order to survive the next two hours alone with Connie.

"He didn't seem mad to me," I said nonchalantly. I wondered how old she was. Probably, truthfully, closer to Noah's age than to mine.

"Normally he's a touch mellower, honey. So—" She smiled wide like I was her friend or something. "What did he want to talk about earlier…when he called you into his office?"

He wanted to kiss me. I almost said the words, really I did. "Family stuff," I said instead. "It was personal."

"Oh. That does seem pretty personal—especially for your second day."

Really? Did she not already know that I was related to Ellie? Minus my sister's short hair and tattoos, we looked a lot alike. It was pretty obvious. "Ellie's my older sister. I've known Noah since I was about eight years old. So, yes, it was pretty personal."

Connie didn't try to make small talk again after that.

chapter **11:**

NOAH

I'd kissed her. Well, sort of. It had been a closed mouth, barely one second
long kiss you saved for your grandma on Sundays. But nevertheless,
despite its brevity and G-rating, that one little kiss might have been my
undoing. I knew I liked her; I just hadn't expected the burst of emotion that
shot through my chest as my lips connected with hers.

Was it protectiveness or lust or *more*?

I didn't even care. I only wanted more.

The minutes ticked by but two o'clock eventually came around. I was
outside pulling weeds. *No, shit.* I would have gone home sooner or taken a
long lunch, but I couldn't leave while Georgie was still working. I'd been
watching the time but had been momentarily sidetracked by the sudden
groundskeeper job I'd given myself. I normally saved this sort of thing for
the occasional flair of my so-called 'OCD'—when my need for order
mixed with my insomnia and I found myself awake with nothing to do at
five in the morning. At least, when that sort of thing happened, it happened
in the early morning hours when it wasn't so blistering hot. The afternoon
sun was torture, but it became bearable when the most fucking gorgeous
girl snuck up on me.

"There you are," Georgie said. "Connie thought maybe you'd left
already. I guess not."

"Still here," I replied, squinting against the sun to get a better look at
her. Hangovers and the sun never mixed well, but seeing her instantly

made up for it all. Her dark hair fell over her shoulders and The Presidential Swing American flag t-shirt she wore fit her body exceptionally well. Ellie had designed the t-shirts for our employees, and they were corny as hell. Secretly we'd both had a big laugh over the fact that we had the power to actually make people wear such a horrendously backwoods redneck t-shirt. But dammit, Georgie could wear whatever the hell she wanted and still look gorgeous.

"I was kind of waiting for you," I admitted.

"Yeah?" She smiled but it quickly faded and was replaced with nervousness. It was the same nervousness she'd exhibited when she came into my office earlier. "Did you need to see me about something?"

I stood, peeling the gardening gloves off my fingers. My hands were sweaty. I was sweaty. Or I might have grabbed her and kissed her right then because I sure as hell didn't like the way she phrased that question or the way she was fidgeting with the hem of her shirt. "Yes, I wanted to see you. But when you put it that way it makes my stomach churn. I wanted to see you because *I* wanted to see you—not as your boss but only as me. I had fun working with you earlier. It was light. It was casual. It was just us. That's how I want it to always be when we work together. Don't be nervous. It's just me."

Her fidgeting stopped, and she met my stare rather fiercely. "Trust me, the boss thing isn't an issue right now. It's the Noah Clark, pulling weeds, sweat trickling down your neck, white t-shirt clinging to your abs thing that's the problem. Sorry if I find that—". She waved her hand, motioning to my body. "Distracting. Meanwhile, I'm over here in my new flag t-shirt—the one I know for a fact you and Ellie designed to be as dorky as humanly possible. So...thanks for that, *boss*."

I could not stop the big-ass grin that took over my face. She was too fucking adorable for her own good, especially now that I'd gotten her a little riled up. "Spend the rest of the day with me," I demanded. "Please. It's what I wanted to see you about—why I've been waiting out here for you."

It took her a few long seconds, but she slowly nodded. "Okay."

"Thank Christ. It's too damn hot for this." Being a touch dramatic, especially for me, I tossed my gloves on the ground and kicked aside the shovel I'd been using to dig up weeds. "I'll finish this later. Or never. Let's go." I stretched out my hand for hers. And she took it. She locked her fingers with mine, not even the least bit concerned that my palms were somewhat sweaty. Words completely failed me. I was not sure why this girl had so much power over me—but she did.

We started back toward the main building, saying nothing. Once we reached the door, I left her and hurried inside. Grabbing my helmet and jacket out of the office, I mumbled a quick goodbye to Connie and the other employee now working. Then in a flash, I returned to Georgie. I nodded in the direction of my bike and led her across the parking lot. My heart was beating out of control and all I wanted was to get out of here. I set the helmet down on the seat and held up the jacket for her to wear. "Put this on. I know it's hot, but if a giant dragonfly hits your skin it stings like a bitch."

She narrowed her pretty blue eyes up at me. "What about you?"

"I'm a man. I can handle the pain."

"Okay. Fine," she said, smiling. Then she let me help her into the jacket.

I handed her the helmet next. "This too."

She put up no argument about the helmet which was a good thing because there was no chance in hell I would have let her within ten feet of my motorcycle without it. I sat down and she, using my shoulders as a prop, climbed on behind me.

Shorts. She was wearing fucking shorts.

I'd touched her legs before—when snuggling almost turned into something more the other night. However, this was different. Somehow more intimate. Her legs hugged the sides of my hips, while my hands itched with the need to grab them and pull them tighter to me.

"I've never been on a motorcycle before," she said. "Where do I put my hands?"

Shit. My mind went straight to the gutter. I swallowed hard. "You can hold onto me."

Lightly her fingers touched my sides—like she was too afraid to hold me properly. But then something changed. She scooted her hips flesh against my backside and wrapped her arms around my stomach.

Dammit. This wasn't going to work.

"How did you get here today?" I suddenly needed to know. "Um. Did you drive? Do you have a car? Maybe we should take your car. That would be much safer."

"Noah," she whined. "Just go. I'm burning up in this jacket."

"I don't even know where the hell I'm going."

Smooth, Noah. Real Smooth.

"Can we go by my house so I can change?" she asked.

"Yes," I said. "I need a shower anyway." An ice cold shower.

* * *

The speed limit was thirty-five. I drove fifteen. We reached her house where she handed me back my jacket and helmet. Then we went inside.

And, of course, every single member of her family was home and hanging out in the living room. The real-estate family business thing meant that sometimes this was the case. I guess it was a slow day and none of them had anything better to do. Including Ellie, who sat on the sofa with a tub of Ben and Jerry's in hand. Whatever. Either way, I expected a reaction out of someone—*anyone*. Georgie and I had just shown up. Together. Alone. Randomly. And no one so much as batted an eye. No one noticed it as anything out of the norm.

"Hi, sweetie," Mrs. Turner said to Georgie, glancing up from her laptop. She sat at the kitchen counter—her usual spot for working. "How was your second day?"

"Fine," Georgie answered. She was doing that 'fidget with the hem of her shirt' thing again.

Mrs. Turner smiled brightly at her daughter. She was generally a happy person, but this smile seemed forced. I could tell everything—Ben's death and Georgie's suicide attempt—weighted down on her, despite how effectively she was hiding it all. "Anything exciting happen?"

Georgie shook her head and avoided glancing in my direction. "Nothing much. I'm just going to go change," she said.

Nothing much? I was not sure if her words were meant for me or for her mother. But she spoke quickly and then moved for the stairs, disappearing from the living room.

"So," Ellie said through a mouth full of ice cream. "Rhett is at Chancy's. *Again*. Apparently, according to Luce who called me earlier, he's making a big scene of not leaving. *Again*. Want to head over there with me? I mean, you're better at dealing with his moods than I am." She sighed, taking another bite of ice cream. "God, he was so annoying last night when I picked you two up. He kept going on and on about some random girl. Anyway, what do think? Go with me. Pretty please."

"Um." Realizing now that I was lingering at the edge of the room, I took a few steps toward the couch. "Fine, I guess."

"I'll invite Georgie too. Hope you're okay with that." Ellie winked at me.

That reminded me that I needed to shower. I excused myself and went downstairs. Georgie's casual words, *nothing much,* kept repeating in my head. Technically, 'nothing much' had happened between us today. But it felt like something more to me.

I undressed, stepped into the shower while the water was still lukewarm, and took my time washing off. I still had those butterfly things happening in my stomach. They hadn't left me all day. Mostly I wondered how the rest of the afternoon would play out. Would Georgie come with us to Chancy's? Would she fit in with my friends? Because, other than the Turners, these people were the only family I had. I wanted her to like them. But mostly, I just wanted her to like me.

"Noah," Ellie yelled, beating on the bathroom door. I was standing, absentmindedly under the shower head, the water running down my body. "Let's go, princess. Georgie and I are ready and waiting on your ass. Save some water for the rest of the planet, please."

"Yeah, yeah. I'm coming," I yelled back. Cutting off the water, I stepped out of the shower and dried quickly. I pulled on a pair of clean boxers and a fresh pair of pants, but a small knock stopped me cold. Ellie never knocked; she only pounded. A second later, Georgie opened the door and slipped inside the bathroom.

Thoroughly fucking surprised, I nearly fell backward into the tub.

"Hey," she said softly. "Is this okay? Me going with you and Ellie to Chancy's. I feel like I'm intruding. Ellie said it was okay but if it's not then I'll stay home. No big deal."

"Do you want to stay home?" I asked, pulling my shirt on over my head.

"I don't know," she answered with a shrug.

The bathroom was steamy, tiny, and forcing us closer together. She'd changed into a short-ass skirt and a lacy tank-top thing. Both way too damn fancy for Chancy's. The men there were going to eat her alive. *I* wanted to eat her alive. How easy would it be to grab her waist, lift her up onto the bathroom sink, push that little skirt of hers up, and find out if she tasted as sweet as she looked?

Holy shit. Stop thinking about her like that, Noah.

Summoning all my control, I managed to keep my hands to myself.

"I said I wanted to spend the day with you," I told her. "I meant that. We can do something else instead."

"No." Shaking her head, she reached for the door knob. "Let's go. I just needed to make sure it was okay with you."

And as quickly as she'd snuck into the bathroom, she snuck out.

* * *

"I've never been to Chancy's," Georgie confessed. "Am I dressed okay?"

"Rule Number Sixty-Two," Ellie said from the driver's seat. "As long as you *own* whatever you wear, you can wear whatever the hell you want. And right now you look smoking, kiddo. Own it."

"Okay then," she muttered. "Um, what does number sixty-two mean?"

"It's a little game Noah and I play sometimes. We assign random numbers to rules—the important ones always get 'Rule Number One.' But, like I said the other day, Rule Number One: There are no rules. And I seriously do mean that."

I sighed. No one on the planet could follow Ellie's logic. I played along with her games, but mostly they made zero sense. But Georgie nodded in agreement, as if she understood perfectly.

The three of us were all riding in Ellie's small two-door Civic. Instead of driving like I usually did, I'd handed the keys over to Ellie because, truthfully, my emotions were still going haywire, and I didn't need to be the one driving. She'd understood, picking up on my silent plea, and hopped in the driver's seat without making a big deal of it. *Thank Christ.* And being the gentleman that I wasn't but wanted to be around Georgie, I'd sat in the tiny backseat. Meanwhile, my leg had a mind of its own and would not stop bobbing up and down.

Was she dressed okay? Fuck, no.

From my view in the back, I could see that tiny skirt of hers riding up her thigh. Not only that, she'd since added cowboy boots to her outfit. So was she dressed okay? Yes, she was fucking stunning. But was I going to be able to make it through the rest of the day without getting into a fight or taking her in the bathroom. Unlikely. I squeezed my fingers into my thighs, wishing like hell my mind would stop thinking such dirty thoughts about her.

It was a short drive to Chancy's since everything around here was a short drive. We exited the car and headed for the doors. Instead of fidgeting with the hem of her shirt, Georgie now fidgeted with her skirt. Her eyes kept flickering in my direction. Several feet separated us on our walk across the parking lot. I'd been nervous as hell all morning. But suddenly, a calm and new sense of confidence washed over me.

She. Was. Mine.

At least, I wanted her to be mine. We were different ages—I didn't care. We were at different stages in our lives—I didn't care. The circumstances of us coming together weren't ideal—I didn't care.

I decided right then and there that she was going to be mine, in every way possible, and that was all that mattered. Fuck the rest of the world. And fuck my 'no wild cards policy.' I'd risk it all for this girl. Give up all the control in my life for her. And it was as simple as that.

So why the hell wasn't she already tucked in close under my arm?

I quickened my pace, closing the small gap between us. I wanted to walk into Chancy's *together* so that no other soul in the building questioned who she belonged with. So Georgie didn't question it either.

Wrapping an arm over her shoulders, I pulled her close against me. At my sudden touch, she sucked in a small, surprised breath but didn't push me away or resist my gesture. On the contrary, she relaxed against my chest—the same way she had a tendency to do during the times we'd shared a bed together.

"You're beautiful, sweetheart," I said softly against her temple, low enough so that Ellie's eavesdropping ears couldn't hear. "I'm not sure how that fact didn't consume me before, but it's all that consumes me now. I need you to stay close to me tonight."

I looked down at her, wanting to be sure she'd heard me. She had. I knew she'd heard because her cheeks were a nice, rosy pink shade. Damn, it was the sweetest thing—knowing I had been the one to put that blush on her cheeks.

The three of us entered the bar. And it was a packed house. Tourist season meant you could never quite tell when or where the vacationers would all decide to flock. Today it seemed Chancy's was the hotspot in town. *Had Rhett had any luck finding his girl since yesterday?* Actually, for as crowded as the place was, now I started wondering if we'd even find him.

"I'm gonna get some drinks," Ellie said, nodding toward the shoulder-to-shoulder crowd around the bar. "You two go find Rhett."

Weaving through the people, with Georgie still tucked close against my side, I quickly located Rhett—the thoughtful bastard had a table saved for us. He and Luce, plus our mutual friend Trevor, sat in a spot on the cusp between the indoor seating and the outdoor deck. I pulled out a plastic chair for Georgie and took the seat opposite her.

"This is Georgie—Georgina," I said making introductions. I had no idea if she'd already met any of them or not. "She's Ellie's sister.

Georgie—this is Trevor, Luce, and Rhett."

"Nice to meet you all," Georgie said with an easy smile on her face. Obviously, she was much better at meeting new people than I was. "A lot of people call me Gina, but whatever is fine."

Gina? Hell, I didn't even know that. I preferred Georgie.

Georgie reached across the table, shaking each person's hand in turn. Rhett was the last in the circle and as she let his hand go, he said, "If whatever is fine…then I think I'll give you a *special* nickname."

"Oh, no. Not again," Luce whined. "He does this with everyone he meets—gives them a random, yet cute, nickname. And, seriously, he's gonna call you that nickname *forever*. He does it so he doesn't have to remember anyone's name." She nudged Rhett in the ribs. "Jerkoff, maybe you should stop doing that…since it worked out *so* well with the last girl."

"What's your nickname?" Georgie asked Luce.

Luce shook her head. "Nope. It's too awful to share."

"I'll share it. It's Lollipop," Trevor deadpanned. "She hates it."

"Trevor," Luce moaned, slumping back in her chair with her arms crossed tightly over her chest. "Not fair. No one needs to know that. It's embarrassing."

"It's kind of cute. Random yet cute," Georgie said politely, but then she unexpectedly burst out laughing. "Sorry. No," she said, catching her breath. "I lied. It's a really bad nickname. So…what's Noah's nickname then?"

"Hell, no," Rhett said. "I never give nicknames to guys. Only girls."

"Okay, fine." Georgie sat up in her chair a little straighter. "Luce can't be the only one with a horrible nickname. I'm ready for mine—since your poor brain doesn't have the capacity to remember Georgie."

"Oh, trust me, my 'poor brain' will forever remember your name. This one—" Rhett nodded in my direction. "He said your name enough times yesterday that it will be forever burned on my cortex."

I had? The easy smile left Georgie's face and a different one—a fucking adorable one—replaced it. "He did?"

"Yes," Rhett answered. "Annoying, right? Okay. Nickname. Nickname. What will your nickname be?" He rubbed a hand over his shortly shaved head, thinking. "I know." He looked in my direction. "Wild Card."

That fucking bastard. If she was anyone's wild card, she was *my* wild card. And, apparently, I had a big mouth. I must have revealed too much while drinking yesterday. What else had I told him about Georgie?

"Wild Card?" Georgie shrugged. "I guess it's better than Lollipop."

"Hey," Luce said. "I've got a brilliant idea. Want to give the guys nicknames? Rhett's nickname will be Jerkoff. What do you think, Georgie? Want to give Noah a nickname?"

I really wanted to hear this, but Georgie couldn't answer. Because a second later, Ellie came rushing up to our table *without* any drinks.

"Guess who's here?" She collapsed in chair beside her sister, grasping her arm. All eyes were on Ellie. "Oh," she said, noticing that she had the table's full attention. "Nobody you all know. Sorry. Ignore us." Ellie leaned in closer to Georgie.

Rhett, never one to care about Ellie's crazy tangents, obviously didn't care to listen to her now. Instead, he started explain the rules to the made-up drinking game I started yesterday. The rules had vastly expanded in the last twenty-four hours. But I couldn't pay attention to Rhett—not when I so desperately needed to hear what Ellie had to say.

"Sonya Fletcher," she whispered to Georgie. "And she's here with Logan. Your Logan."

chapter **12:**

GEORGINA

You're beautiful, sweetheart. I'm not sure how that fact didn't consume me before, but it's all that consumes me now. I need you to stay close to me tonight.

Noah's words—they had to have been the kindest, gentlest words anyone had ever said to me. And I was having a really good time with him and his friends. They were easy to be around. Granted, I barely knew them, but somehow it felt right—in a way that was brand new to me. I hoped Noah felt it too.

Rhett was a character, a 'wild card' himself, but kind of silly and easy to joke around with. Luce was sweet. She had short brown pixie hair and a hibiscus tattoo that covered the left side of her neck. I liked her immediately. Even Trevor wasn't so bad. The guy had dyed black hair and more ink on him than even my sister, but he smiled easily and his eyes protectively watched over Luce.

Then Ellie muttered, "Your Logan." And the mood at our end of table died in an instant. The softness and easiness on Noah's face dropped. My heart dropped along with it.

"Who's Logan?" Noah asked. His eyes set intently on mine from across the table.

"Duh," Ellie answered before I could speak. "You know who Logan Tyler is. Jeez, sometimes I swear you never pay attention. Logan is her ex-boyfriend."

"No," I muttered—because the last thing I wanted was to lie to Noah. And in my book, even omissions of the truth could be lies. I hadn't realized it, but I guess by not telling Noah about Logan I'd been lying to him. "He's still my boyfriend. Technically. Maybe—" I shrugged, my eyes still locked with Noah's. "Honestly, I don't know what we are. We haven't spoken in four months. It doesn't matter though…because I don't love him."

Noah continued to stare at me for a couple long seconds. Under the table, my hands trembled in my lap. I waited for him to say something—anything. Instead, he said nothing. He stood, his chair scooting along the deck floor boards, and left the table. I watched his back disappear into the crowd.

"Don't worry," Ellie said. Her hand found mine under the table. "He'll be back in ten minutes. I'd bet money on it."

I didn't believe her. I should have told Noah about Logan before now. I should have told him that even though I hadn't officially ended things with Logan, I knew it was over. Now it was too late. Whatever *thing* I had with Noah—well, it was probably over, too.

Keep breathing, I told myself, counting each inhale of air I took. But nothing could have prepared me for how badly this hurt—*because it hurt pretty fucking bad.* And my breathing ritual wasn't doing its trick.

Ellie squeezed my hand tighter. "I'm being serious. He'll be back."

My eyes burned with unshed tears. To make this moment even more embarrassing, Luce noticed something was wrong from the other end of the table. "You okay, babe?" she asked, cutting off her conversation with Rhett and Trevor.

All attention jumped to me.

I nodded, quickly brushing at my eyes. I didn't want Noah's friends to think any less of me. I was already much younger than them. What would they think if I started crying at their table? "I'm fine."

"She's fine," Ellie repeated.

"Quick," Rhett said, resting his elbows on the table and leaning closer to me. "Let's all talk about Noah while he's gone." This mischievous smile lit up his face. "Ready, go."

"Actually, I think I need to use the bathroom." I stood to my feet.

"Me too," Ellie said, following.

"No, I'm okay." When Ellie didn't make a move to sit back down, I firmly said, "Seriously, I'm okay. You don't have to come with me. I'm sure I can use the bathroom by myself. But thanks, though."

"Alright." Ellie tentatively sat back down. She pointed at a line that had formed against the wall, on the other end of the restaurant. "I can see the bathroom from here, kiddo. And the long-ass line you're about to wait in. Wave at me when you get close to the front and I'll come cut."

"Fine," I groaned and set off across the room. The clientele was a mixture of biker-dudes, women who shouldn't be wearing bikinis indoors or ever, and happy-go-lucky tourists. What an odd combo. And if Noah hadn't just left me cold, effectively ripping my heart out of my freaking chest, I might have found that combination amusing. None of my high school friends ever came here. It was—

Speak of the devil.

I never made it to the bathroom. Because a moment later, I ran into Logan Tyler.

* * *

Tall.

Logan was taller than I remembered. He had a very athletic body—even as a boy his arms had definition. He was cocky, confident, and easily one of the most popular boys at our school. *Was.* I had to remind myself that high school was over.

The sparks I used to feel around Logan had faded long ago, and they certainly didn't resurface today. Mostly...seeing him again made me miss my brother. Logan and Ben had been inseparable growing up.

"Logan," I said. "Hi." I glanced over my shoulder, checking to see if Ellie was watching. She was. Like a hawk. And Noah still wasn't back at our table. My gaze returned to Logan. "My sister said she saw you here. With Sonya."

"Yep," he answered. His voice was deep and rich—like always. "We've been hanging out some. Sonya's just over there." He pointed. Sonya was watching us too. I guess she wasn't coming over to say hi though. "She told me she saw you the other day. She told me you were finally home." And suddenly, despite all the eyes on us, he stretched out his arms and gave me a tight hug. "I'm so glad you're okay. You look really healthy. It's good to know you're healthy."

He dropped his grip, and I was surprised to find that the moment wasn't as awkward as I might have imagined. "Thanks, I guess."

"I saw you come in here with Noah Clark."

Holy shit, bring on the awkward. "You did?" Breathing became slightly difficult and I wasn't sure why. Maybe just hearing Noah's name did funny things to me. "And?" I asked, demanding.

"I don't know." He shoved his hands in his pockets, shrugging. "It's weird seeing your ex-girlfriend with anyone. I hear things about Noah. I know he's Ellie's friend and all, but are you sure he's really a good choice for you?"

What the hell did that mean? Not only that—he said ex. So that defined it. "I'm your ex?" I thought aloud. "I never remember us officially ending anything, but I figured the same."

"Well," he answered, his tone turning slightly clipped. "I'm pretty sure *you* officially ended things when you tried to kill yourself."

Ouch.

"Jesus, Logan," I whispered. "Why don't you tell me how you really feel? So that's why you never called me once in the last four months?" Suddenly I wanted to be anywhere else. No. I wanted to be in the guest bedroom at home, snuggled with Noah in the waterbed. That felt like a safe place. This didn't anymore.

"The phone goes both ways," Logan said, but then he seemed to become cognizant of his attitude and his voice softened, if only slightly. "Sorry, you're right. I should have called and checked on you during that time. I should have made an effort to talk to you before today. This is hardly the place." Logan groaned, rubbing a hand over the back of his neck. "It's just—" He shrugged, not finishing his thought.

"Say whatever you need to. Please. We've been sugarcoating with each other long enough."

He nodded. "Okay. Here goes—" He took a breath. "If you really loved me don't you think you'd have wanted to *live*? For me? For us? I know things weren't great this past year. Actually, our relationship had become downright awkward and breaking up probably would have been inevitable either way. I've come to terms with that now. But you could have come to me, confided in me, leaned on me. I lost Ben, too, ya know."

I nodded. He was right about this. I fell out of love with him a long time ago, long before Ben's death. But leaning on him or confiding in him? He wasn't the person I needed. He never fought for me, not when it mattered most. But in truth, I guess I never fought for him either.

"I'm sorry," I said and meant it. "I should have handled things differently. But at the same time, I'm also kind of relieved it's over between us. Breaking up *was* inevitable and maybe if we would have realized that a year ago, things could have been easier—not as forced as they'd become."

He swallowed hard. Then nodded. "Agreed."

"Well then…" I reached out a hand for him to shake.

"A handshake?"

"Friends?" I asked firmly.

He took my hand. "Always, Gina. Always." Then he gave me a hug.

It took an overwhelming amount of effort, but I managed not to cry in that moment. In the very beginning, Logan and I really did have something special. I was not sure where we went wrong. Perhaps the night he cheated on me while drinking at that party. Perhaps I never fully forgave him for that. Or perhaps when Ben left for the Coast Guard and part of the link that held Logan and me together left with him. The answers didn't matter because that chapter of my life was over. But still, I couldn't help feeling a little loss over Logan. And the feeling was compounded by a million due to the fact that I might have just lost Noah, too.

Logan and I exchanged goodbyes and a false promise to call one another more often. Then I sucked in a breath and gathered whatever courage I had left, ready to return to the table with Ellie and no Noah. But as I turned around, I saw the table wasn't quite as empty anymore. Shit. I hesitantly walked across the restaurant—my head and my heart screaming at me.

Because Noah had returned to his seat.

His face was expressionless as his eyes observed me move toward the table—toward him. My emotions were still buzzing out of control from my conversation with Logan. I was not sure if our conversation had made me feel better or worse about the last year of my life. I guess, at the very least, it had settled the argument about my relationship status. But still, either way, I'd already known Logan and I were over. I snuggled with Noah, I shared a kiss with Noah, and I came here with Noah—all of it knowing that there was no one else but Noah.

And then suddenly he stood, leaving his chair before my brain could even comprehend the moment. He had to walk around the table and cut through the crowd of people, but he did it quickly and met me in the middle of the room. He stopped a foot in front of me. A stray piece of his blond hair fell down in his face and his jaw was set hard as he stared down into my eyes.

"You can't be pissed at me," I said, speaking loudly over the noisy room. I really wasn't in the mood for a second break-up conversation. Not that Noah and I were ever even anything to begin with, but I could guess where this was heading. It was over before it had started. But if that were the case, then I was going to give him a piece of my mind—be fierce and reckless like he'd told me to be.

"You can't leave a table in the middle of a conversation," I argued. "So I had some unfinished business to clear up with Logan. So what. It's cleared up now. But on your account—" I pushed a finger into his chest, fired up now. "That was a crappy and hurtful way of ending things with me. Mostly hurtful. I liked you...I mean, *like* you...and you shouldn't—"

He looked down at my finger still pointed into his chest. Realizing how rude I was being, I went to remove my hand. But Noah caught my wrist and pressed my palm flesh against him. My stomach flipped. Because his chest was hard underneath my touch and I could feel the rapid, racing beat of his heart.

I wasn't the only one fired up.

Glancing from his chest up to his face, I desperately needed to see his eyes. Where I expected to find anger, I found a tenderness and a desire no man had ever looked at me with. "I'm not fucking ending anything," he said. And then his hands were suddenly in my hair and his mouth on my mouth. This was no quick kiss like before. This was passion and need and want all bubbling to the surface and breaking free. This was hope and life and a little bit of danger all mixed together as one.

And my own heart raced wildly because of it.

The rest of the world faded into the background and only Noah remained. And seriously—Oh. My. Word. The guy knew how to kiss. His lips were soft and lingering, rushing nothing. The warm feel of his breath mixed with my own, sweet and hot. His hands moved to hold my face still, control his for the taking—and he fully took it. He teased me with his light and tender kiss, making my body ache and scream for more until *he* was ready for more. His tongue trailed the seam of my lips and then, finally, dipped inside my mouth.

Holy shit, Noah!

Part of me was slightly pissed off that this kiss with him hadn't happened sooner. As in *years ago* sooner. Because this one little kiss—it literally rocked my world. He was morphine, and I was an instant addict.

My knees felt weak and I reached up to grasp his shoulders to hold myself steady. A little moan escaped my throat, but I hardly cared because his tongue was caressing mine, playing in a light dance of sorts, and I'd never felt so much energy pumping through my veins.

Far too soon, Noah broke away. He pressed one last quick, tender kiss to my lips and then rested his forehead against mine for a moment. His breathing was heavy. "What the fuck are you doing to me, pretty girl?"

He draped an arm over my shoulder and motioned toward the table. I was at a loss for words and could only lean into him, letting him lead me wherever. We approached the others. And I might have felt embarrassed because surely they all just witnessed that kiss, but I was too stunned to worry about it.

"Well, that was mean," Rhett said to Noah. "I'm trying to nurse a wounded heart here, while you go and rub dirt in my wound." I had no idea what he was talking about. "That was rough, man."

Noah didn't respond. His eyes were on Ellie. She was putting something away in the tan satchel thingy she carried everywhere. "What was that?" Noah asked.

"Um. It might have been my new camera," Ellie answered.

Uh oh.

"You got the camera?" Noah held out his free hand. "Let me see."

Ellie groaned, like a child being reprimanded by a parent. "Seriously, I took like three pictures. It's not a big deal. I don't know why you have to be such a hard ass."

She dug in her bag and pulled out the camera. It was white, compact, and probably cost a hell of a lot of money. Noah dropped his hold on me to flip through it for a moment. Then he handed it back to Ellie.

"You're not going to say anything?" she asked.

"No," he answered, smiling. "But let's get out of here. Rhett—your mystery girl knows where you live. Maybe you should be waiting at the house instead of at this crowded bar."

"Mother Eff!" he shouted, jumping to his feet. "I should have thought of that. Let's go, people."

chapter 13:

NOAH

Frankly, I was mad as hell. Finding out she still might have a boyfriend…well, it metaphorically bulldozed me off my fucking feet. And I should have expected it too. *C'mon, Noah.* She was beautiful and addictive, smart and fun. Why *wouldn't* there already be someone else? I walked away from that table feeling incredibly unsure.

But I didn't get very far.

Leaving Chancy's, I reached the water and that was where I stopped. The Turner's house was only a mile and a half down the beach. On occasion, if Ellie and I were both too drunk to drive, we'd walk to her parents' house from the bar and then crash there. We'd been doing that same routine about once a month ever since we turned twenty-one. It was an easy walk and conveniently my motorcycle was parked there from where I left it earlier.

But my feet would not take me in the direction I urged them to go. It was as simple as that. And one memory kept replaying in my head—the chaste kiss I'd shared with Georgie earlier in my office.

The damn grandma kiss.

I'd had the opportunity to take her in my arms and kiss her like she was meant to be kissed—hot and wet and hard. But I hadn't done that. I'd pussied out earlier. I wasn't pussying out now. So I turned around and marched back across the sand.

Dammit, this girl was more drama than I ever bargained for. It didn't matter, though. Because maybe, just maybe, she was going to be worth *everything* to me.

I retraced my footsteps, followed the stone stairs from the sand up to the deck, and found the table where everyone, minus Georgie, still sat.

"Where is she?" I demanded, not bothering to be polite.

Three blank faces and one smug face stared back at me.

"Nine minutes," Ellie answered, checking her phone. "Booyah. Someone owes me a Coke."

"I'm serious, Ellie. Where is she?"

Ellie took a giant breath. Then she pushed out her chair and made a big show of standing to her feet. That easygoing, shit-eating grin that always lingered on her face—it vanished. And a stern face, one I hardly recognized, replaced it. "Sit your ass down, Noah."

What? "Why?" I asked, leery.

"Because I have something to say."

I could tell she meant business, and Ellie never meant business. So I sat my ass down.

She sat back down in her chair, as well. "Here's the deal," she said, the entire table drawn into our conversation. Even Rhett seemed mesmerized. "You're my best friend, Noah, but Georgie...she's my baby sister. I love you, but if you're not one hundred bazillion percent sure about her—right now, right this moment—then you need to stop this. I can't see her hurt. Never again. It would crush me."

My jaw tightened. "That's not what I want, and you already know that."

"I know," she muttered, her voice cracking. *Shit.* I never meant to upset her.

And then I glanced up. Something across the room caught my eye. Georgie. She was talking to her asshole ex or current boyfriend or whatever the hell he was. I already knew Logan. He was Ben's friend. I just hadn't made the connection between him and Georgie earlier. Before this moment, based on my past knowledge of the guy, I'd already pegged him as a decent man. But he instantly became an asshole in my book— because what kind of fool would give up on such an amazing girl like Georgie? A real fucking asshole—that was who.

Ellie noticed what I'd seen and our conversation ended. All conversation at the table ended. Georgie stood there talking to the asshole for what felt like forever. I didn't charge across the room or do anything stupid—because, frankly, that had never been my style. I knew when to shut my mouth, and I knew when to bide my time. And I also realized I knew Georgie a little better than I thought.

At work earlier, I'd spent a full thirty minutes studying her, memorizing that sexy little body of hers. When she felt comfortable, she had an easygoing, playful way about her. Not too unlike Ellie. But the Georgie I observed now had her arms crossed tightly over his stomach and a rigid posture. She was wildly uncomfortable and possibly in pain. And every ounce of my being, every bone in my body, tingled with the need to go save her—to interrupt her conversation with the asshole, swoop her up in my arms, and just carry her out of this place.

I was about to go do exactly that because I couldn't take another nanosecond of this torture. But then she jetted out her hand, and he shook it. Well, that was a fucking relief. A handshake was about the last thing I'd ever want Georgie to offer me. It spoke volumes. It told me all I needed to know.

Logan gave her a small, cringe-worthy hug, and they parted ways. Georgie back in my direction, and Logan off in the other direction. And as Georgie turned around, I noticed a little falter in her step when she spotted me across the room. Heat scorched through my body as her eyes collided with mine.

That moment had come—the moment where I couldn't go another minute without knowing what those sweet, plump lips of hers would taste like.

"I'm one hundred bazillion percent sure," I whispered to Ellie, standing, while my eyes stayed focused on Georgie. I left the table, crossed the room, and gave her the kiss my whole damn body was aching for.

That was almost three hours ago.

Now, with her head resting on my thigh and her long hair fanned across my lap, Georgie lay curled up against me on the living room sofa. I brushed my fingers over her silky brown hair. I'd been wanting to touch it for days now, maybe even longer. She'd fallen asleep about two episodes ago during the *Seinfeld* marathon the five of us had started after leaving Chancy's and coming back to my house. But the sun was sinking outside and it was still my day to work. I needed to get back to The Swing to help out during our busiest time of the day. Which, unfortunately, had to be right the fuck now.

With a sigh, I gently lifted her head and tried to move off the couch without waking her. No such luck. She sat up, narrowing her eyes at me, and briefly stretched her arms above her head. "How long was I out?" she asked.

"Not long. I have to go, though. Come talk with me in my room for a quick minute first?"

She nodded and stood to follow me, her cheeks turning a cute shade of pink at my request. Ellie whistled as we crossed in front of her and left the room together. The others were too into the show to care. She followed me down the dark hallway and into my room. I couldn't tell if she was being shy or if she wasn't saying anything because she'd only just woken up. I flipped on the light and led her inside.

Her eyes took in her surroundings. My room was neat—yes, I was a neat freak. I went for my dresser, needing something to do. There I found a rubber band and quickly pulled my hair back. I pocketed my car keys and cellphone, then glanced up in the mirror only to catch Georgie watching me closely. I froze and stared at her for a moment. This weird expanding feeling happened in my chest. It was the same feeling that kept happening when I was with her.

Clinging to the edge of my dresser, I gripped my fingers into the wood—because her hair was a little ruffled and her pretty blue eyes sleepy. She was sexy as fuck and having her alone in my room wasn't helping. I never usually let anyone into my room. I liked to keep my personal space personal. But I kept making exceptions for this girl and what was worse, I no longer cared that I was. The blood roaring through my veins was finding its way south. I needed to say something, anything, before I lost complete control here. My fingers dug harder into the wood, but not a single, damn word came out of my mouth.

Did she feel this too?

She exhaled slowly and broke some of the tension by speaking first. "Your room is nice. It's very clean."

"I have a problem with that. Come here." My voice came out rougher than normal. She stood too far away, and I needed her closer.

"You have a problem with what?" she asked and walked across the room.

"With cleaning."

"That sounds like a good kind of problem." As she approached, I managed to unclamp my hands from the dresser so that I could turn around and hold her instead. My grip settled on the sides of her waist, and I pulled her against my groin. My dick was hard and straining against my jeans. We'd entered very dangerous territory. Alone. In my room. Me hard as a rock and losing control. But mostly, I just needed her near me.

"Ellie and Rhett both love my *problem*. I'm their damn maid, whether they want me to be or not. But for me, actually, it's just…time-consuming." I'd never dared admit I had a problem until this moment, but the honest to God truth was that I did spend way too much of my free time cleaning and re-cleaning. I sighed, wishing I'd kept my mouth shut. "Anyway, sorry I brought that up. I didn't bring you back here to burden you with my shit. I just wanted a moment alone with you before I had to go back to work."

"You can burden me with whatever."

I reached up to brush away a strand of her hair that had fallen in her face.

"Seriously," she said, pulling away from me and sitting down on the edge of my bed. "It's not like I don't notice how everyone is careful around me. My mom has been super, sickeningly sweet ever since my suicide attempt. She used to tell me, to the point of constantly annoying me, exactly what she thought about every little thing I did. Good or bad. Now she's careful with everything she says. Dad too. Even Ellie kind of—in her own way. It's nice. I love that everyone is trying so hard to make me comfortable. I know they all love me, and I'm sure with time everything will go back to normal, but if you want to burden me with your shit then do it. Because, seriously, I'm not as fragile as everyone thinks."

A smile crept over my lips. When she got fired up it was the most fucking adorable thing in the world. "Okay," I said. "Yes, I spend a lot of my time cleaning. But it's not so much about everything being clean, but about everything being orderly."

"What does *orderly* mean?"

I really didn't want her to think less of me. In. Any. Way. Because I loved the way she looked at me. Like right this moment—her big eyes stared up at me as she waited on whatever I might say, like we were having a much more interesting and pleasant conversation than we really were. But why not tell her? Maybe it would make her feel more normal to know how fucked-up I truly was. "It means I keep everything in my environment immaculately clean because it brings me a sense of calmness. Same goes for work and my personal life. I like things my way. I'm like this because my childhood was complete chaos and I crave the opposite now. And the worst part is, I know there should be a problem there somewhere, but mostly I'm fine with the way I am. Aside from the time-consuming part."

"And your nightmares?" she asked, not missing a beat. "How do they fit in?"

I swallowed hard. I'd forgotten she knew about those also. "Completely separate problem."

"But am I still helping that some? I mean, being your snuggle-buddy and all."

I couldn't help but smile. "Yes." More than she'd ever know.

"Good." She dropped her arms to her sides, tucking her fingers under the edges of her thighs. Seeing the image of her sitting there on my bed in that skirt of hers had my stomach doing summersaults. "But Noah," her voice softly said, "if I'm ever doing anything that interferes with your *orderly* thing then you have to tell me."

But that was the thing—for the first time in my life, I wanted the interference. I had my rules and I had my walls and I wanted to let her smash each one of them away. Only her. I didn't respond to her request but instead moved across the short distance that separated us, took her face in my hands, and pressed my lips to hers. I claimed her mouth with mine, taking exactly what I wanted. She tasted so damn sweet, and she opened up to me so easily.

"I have to go," I said, breaking away from her perfect mouth. I needed to get away from her before I completely lost my shit. "I'll see you, in bed, later tonight."

* * *

Normally I enjoyed work. I was proud of my business and how efficiently Ellie and I ran everything. But tonight, for as busy as we were, the time dragged. I'd never in my life told anyone the things I'd told Georgie earlier. And as I sat in the back office, running over the day's numbers, she was all I could focus on. *Why had I opened up to her so easily?* Maybe because I felt like she actually listened when I spoke. Or maybe because whenever her blue eyes stared in my direction there was zero judgment reflected back in them. I liked those things about her, and it didn't hurt that she was something straight out of a fucking dream as well.

In high school, I'd been *that* kid. The one everyone whispered about and secretly feared would one day bring a bomb in his backpack to blow up the school. I had a mean, abusive uncle waiting at home to tell me exactly the kind of fuck-up he thought I was each night. He was the only person I had left in the world. I had no friends, no real family, and no hope of a better future. I was lost, drowning in hate and chaos, until Ellie found me—her friendship saved my life.

When I saw Georgie bleeding out on that bathroom floor, maybe I saw a little of myself in her, a little of that lost kid who wore black eyeliner, trench coats, and hated himself. I saved her life that night. But I hadn't counted on everything that had happened since. Part of me felt like Georgie was saving me, all over again, the way Ellie had back in high school. But this was more, this was deeper, and I hadn't even realized I still needed saving.

I took a breath, trying to pull myself out of my thoughts. I didn't want to make sense of it all. I just wanted to let whatever was happening with

Georgie happen. It felt good so far, so why start questioning it?

Staring out my office window, the one that overlooked the miniature golf course, my eyes raked over the people left golfing. It was past eleven, we were officially closed, and all I had left to do was wait on those still golfing to finish up before I could head back to my girl.

And that was when I spotted her. Rhett's girl. The mystery girl. The blonde. *Holy shit!* I jumped to my feet, dashing out of the office, determined to talk to this girl before she disappeared again. I still had no earthly clue how I knew her, but Rhett hadn't dropped his infatuation since he'd slept with her, and I couldn't let her slip away without saying something for my friend.

Dashing across the course, jumping over the mini Mount Rushmore, I leaped right in the path of Little Miss Mystery Girl. I mentally started running over the possibilities of where I might know her. Was she a past employee? No, I'd remember. Was she someone I went to high school with? No, she seemed younger than me.

"Noah," she gasped, startled by my sudden appearance. "You scared the shit out of me."

How the fuck did she know my name? She wasn't alone either. She was with some random guy—a guy with dark hair and more piercings than even the people in my crowd rolled with. I think she was on a date, one I'd just interrupted, and the fucker looked like he was ready to beat my ass for it too. I hadn't meant to spring over Teddy Roosevelt's head, nearly toppling the girl, acting like a jealous ex-boyfriend.

I caught my breath and took a step backward.

"How do you know my name?" I asked.

"I remember you from the other night," she answered.

"Oh." I glanced at the guy who hadn't stopped glaring at me. He needed to calm the hell down. I hadn't done a damn thing here. I brought my attention back to the blonde. "Sorry I interrupted your game, but Rhett Morgan has been looking for you. You know, my roommate."

She brushed her hair over one shoulder, letting out a little chuckle. "Yeah, I've already heard—from you and about five others now. It's a small town. Word gets around. Did it ever occur to people that maybe I don't want to be found?" She stepped onto the putting green, lining up her club with her golf ball. "It's called a 'one-night stand' for a reason."

Mr. Three Lip Rings groaned. "Seriously, do you have to say that shit in front of me?" he whined. "No brother wants to hear about how his little sister is fucking the town *man-whore*."

"Shut up, John." Unfazed, she swung her putter and sunk her ball into the hole in one easy shot. Then she turned her attention back to me. "Tell Rhett I had an amazing night. He was sweet—" *Sweet?* Rhett Morgan wasn't sweet. Was she high? "And I never meant to hurt him. But one night was all I wanted." She shrugged, effectively dismissing me.

"Fine. I'll tell him," I answered, walking off. If she didn't reciprocate Rhett's feelings then I wasn't going to stand around and argue. Still, now I was beyond pissed that I had to be the one to break the bad news to my friend. I'd never seen him so focused on one girl in his life. This was going to crush him.

Entering the main building, I glanced one last time over my shoulder at Rhett's girl and her brother. None of this explained why she looked familiar. And maybe she had a brother who looked like an axe-murdering drug-dealer, (though I shouldn't be judging since others did the same thing far too often with me) but this girl exuded an innocence her crass words didn't match and I couldn't make sense of it all.

And then, finally, I remembered where I knew her from.

I'd seen her once before, but her hair had been brown then. I'd seen her at Ben's funeral—crying harder than anyone in the room.

chapter **14:**

GEORGINA

I woke a little before the sun to a very handsome man in bed with me. When I'd fallen asleep the night before, I'd fallen asleep alone.

I certainly wasn't alone now.

Somehow I'd ended up with my leg hooked high over my intruder's waist, his hand gently resting on my ass, and my face pressed against his chest. My unconscious self must have been clinging to the guy all night, like her own personal life-sized teddy bear, and I probably should have felt embarrassed for that, but I was way too ecstatic to care. Noah could crawl into bed with me anytime he liked, and I'd never get tired of it.

Breathing in deep, I inhaled the scent of him. Jeez, he even smelled amazing, too, like clean laundry, summer sunshine, and Noah all mixed as one. Sometimes I forgot our age difference, and sometimes it was hard to ignore. Like right now. He radiated a masculinity, a maturity, a confidence even in his sleep that other guys my own age just couldn't even compare to. Maybe that was less about his age and more about *him*. Either way, it was incredibly sexy—*he* was incredibly sexy. I kind of loved the fact that he could physically snap me in two and the fact that I knew he never would.

I nestled a little closer into his chest, my fingers tracing gently over the contours of his abs. This close contact made my chest feel all gooey and warm inside, and I took advantage of this small opportunity to touch him while he slept. *Because what if these opportunities were only temporary?*

"Damn," he muttered. "You're sweet as fuck to wake up to."

I froze, my heart going off like a jackhammer against my ribs. I never meant to wake him. "Sorry, Noah."

"Don't apologize." His voice was rough with sleep. His fingers on my ass gripped tighter. "I missed having you in my arms yesterday. So, explore all you want, pretty girl. It's nice. It's making me hard, but it's really fucking nice."

Burying my face in his chest, I hid the giant grin he'd just put on my lips. "Sorry for that too," I mumbled against him.

"Nope." He grabbed my hips and pulled me on top of him. "Stop apologizing. I like it, and I like you. Let's do something crazy today."

My fingers dug into the hard muscles of his chest. I stared down at him as he gazed up at me. "Like what?" I asked, swallowing hard. What could be crazier than this? I was straddling Noah, the feel of his erection pressing against me. Only a few layers of cotton separated us, and I desperately wanted to remove those layers. I wiggled against him, trying to gain some friction.

He sat up, cupping the sides of my face, kissing me so deep that I felt it over every inch of my body. Only when I was breathless and slightly trembling did he break away. Damn, he was a good kisser—soft yet demanding. And the way he liked to linger, take his time, and savor every second...*wow*. Double wow. I knew that if he ever touched me, *really* touched me, then I'd surely turn straight to putty in his hands.

"Something that reminds us we're alive," he whispered, tracing his thumb over my bottom lip, dipping it inside the depth of my mouth for the briefest of moments. "Something happened to me when I found you on that floor, Georgie. Something that resonated deep inside me. I can't shake it. I can't explain it. But whatever happened, it's part of me now. *You're* part of me now. So, will you come with me? Will you trust me?"

"Yes," I breathed. Forget needing him to touch me; I was already putty in his arms.

"Good," he answered, moving from our little cocoon of sheets and pillows. He stretched out a hand and helped me climb out of the bed after him.

"Do I need to change out of my pajamas?"

"Nope."

He tugged on my hand, leading me out of the guestroom, across the basement living room, and toward the door. *We were leaving?* The sun had barely started to rise, and I didn't even have shoes on my feet. Where could we possibly be going so early in the morning? The beach? If that were the case, then I still wasn't sure I was fully ready to face all my demons.

"Noah," I whispered, my heart beating wildly in my chest. "Wait."

"Yeah?" He stopped and turned.

Most of his hair had fallen lose from the ponytail he wore, blond stands tucked behind his ears. He had on his plaid pajama pants—the ones, I realized, that he must be keeping permanently at my house. They hung low on his hips, but all I could focus on was the sincerity on his face. Looking into his eyes, I found I trusted him wholeheartedly. So it didn't matter where he was taking me.

"Never mind," I answered.

Even if he was leading me to the beach, then I was going to let him.

But he didn't take me down to the beach. He took me to the wooden gate of the neighbor's backyard fence. 'Sol Mate' was the rental property next door. Unlatching the gate, he gestured for me to follow him—a wicked grin playing on his lips. "It's empty this week," he whispered. "I noticed last night. And they have the biggest pool. Want to get in with me?"

Opening the gate revealed the biggest freaking pool I'd ever seen in my life. How did I *not* know this was here? 'Sol Mate' was a modest sized beach house, but my eyes quickly discovered that it had a pool fit for a king…or a party bus full of kings. There was even a waterfall.

"It's beautiful," I said.

"Yeah, I think so too," Noah responded, his whiskey eyes on me instead of the pool. "C'mon." He tugged on my arm, pulling me through the gate, which he quickly latched behind us. "Want to get in with me?" he repeated, his voice a little uneven this time.

Like any sane woman would turn down a determined Noah. "Sure," I breathed.

"Naked?" he added.

He said the word and I nearly tripped over my own feet, straight onto the fancy-ass tile that surrounded the pool. My stomach instantly turned into a swirly mess. Noah watched me carefully, waiting on my answer. I couldn't speak. I couldn't breathe. My body was on fire—desire pooling deep in my belly from just talking about all this.

He padded across the tile and dipped his foot into the water. "It's only a little cold, pretty girl. Say yes. It's just me."

"Yes," I whispered, realizing that nothing else mattered. Just Noah and my sudden and desperate need to see him without his clothes. It was now daylight. We were trespassing. But I didn't care. Because I wanted this. I *needed* this. "You first," I muttered. "You're gonna have to go first."

His smile grew. *How could he be so casual about this? Was this something he did all the time?* And then he did it! He took off his *freaking* clothes! He started with his shirt. Tugging at the back, he yanked his white t-shirt over his head in one quick motion, exposing his chest. Jeez. The definition, the perfect lines…I'd seen it before, but that didn't make it any less overwhelming. I was forever going to dream of his chest. But I hardly had the time to fully appreciate anything because, gripping his plaid waistband, he pushed down his pants.

Oh. Holy. Shit. He wasn't wearing any underwear. His erection sprang free, as if it were reaching out for me, and Noah didn't even flinch. He was perfectly comfortable being one hundred percent buck naked in front of me. I guess, when you had a body like his, there was no need for fear. "Your turn," he said and nodded in my direction. "Go slow for me, sweetheart."

My knees went weak.

I wasn't sure if I could do this. But then I realized something—if I'd succeeded in taking my own life four months ago, then I'd be dead and this moment wouldn't exist. Life was fragile. It could be harsh, and it could be unfair. But it could also be pretty damn amazing. None of us knew how many days or even how many minutes we had left on this planet—why not take advantage of every single second? I had so many regrets about everything else, about my last conversation with Ben, about my failed suicide attempt, that there was no chance in hell that I wanted to let this moment fall into my pile of regrets as well. And I knew, without a doubt, that if I didn't live this experience to its absolute fullest then I'd regret the hell out of it for the rest of my life.

So...

With my eyes locked on Noah's, I tugged my shirt over my head. I hadn't worn a bra to bed, meaning this small action exposed my breasts to him and to the empty backyard. Even early in the morning, the North Carolina air was hot and humid, and yet, my nipples were painfully hard as if I were standing in the middle of snowstorm.

"Mother*fucker*," Noah swore.

I never had the chance to finish undressing. Noah cut across the short distance that separated us. Maybe this wasn't as *casual* for him as I initially thought. Because his breaths were short, choppy, and completely affected. Not to mention, the slight tremble I felt in his touch as his hands moved to grip the sides of my arms.

His eyes were penetrating and his jaw tense as he whispered, "I don't think I have the control to continue this. I thought I did, but seeing you naked is too damn much for me to bear. If we get in that pool then I don't know what will happen. I've never felt something this intense for anyone. My body is screaming at me. I'm losing my fucking mind here, and I don't know how to handle that."

The raw vulnerability, the panic, and the desire written all over his face was overwhelming. To say the least. Whatever I felt for him, he felt it just as strong for me. But these feelings were something I wanted to embrace not shove away. I needed him to embrace everything with me.

So, I pressed my palms against his chest and gently pushed, forcing him to take one step backward. His grip dropped from my arms, confusion and shock filling his face. He hadn't expected me to push him away. But I wasn't pushing him away—the opposite, actually.

Now that I had the space to do so—slowly, like he'd asked—I finished undressing. I inched my cotton shorts down my legs, exposing the black lace panties I had on underneath. A breath of air hissed through Noah's teeth.

Last night, knowing Noah might be back to snuggle with me, I'd gone to bed prepared. My panties were see-through and sexy. I'd picked them hoping that if he saw me in them, maybe he'd see me as a woman and not as someone younger than him. Six years felt like a lot to me—but as I threw all caution out the window and slipped my black panties down my thighs, I could tell by the way Noah was watching me that the 'age thing' was the last thing on his mind.

"Lose control with me," I whispered, standing before him just as naked as he was, still stuck in my own personal snowstorm. "You said you wanted to do something that lets us know we're alive. Losing your fucking mind *is* that feeling. I've never felt more alive than I do right this moment."

"Same here," he answered, his voice gritty and low, his hands settling on my hips.

And then something caught my eye—a pair of little kid's water shoes. They were pink and left laying haphazardly beside the edge of the pool. "Noah," I whispered just as he drew me close against his body. "There are shoes over there."

"What?"

He turned to see what I meant, and then suddenly a light flipped on inside the house.

Noah groaned and moved faster than I've ever seen anyone move. Bending quickly, he gathered whatever clothes were at our feet, stood back up to press them over my naked chest, forcing me to hold them, and then he bent back over and lifted me clear off feet. I squealed as he flung me over his shoulder like a rag doll. His hand gripped my ass cheek to hold me tightly against him and he took off sprinting—out of the yard and down the beach as fast possible.

My view was superb. I knew there had to be people out on the beach—the elderly residents of Kill Devil Hills loved to take early morning walks along the shore. And I knew we had to be making the most epic scene ever. But all I really saw was Noah's fine ass, running in motion, carrying me away. He cut into a grass covered sand dune, dropped to his knees, and helped me slip down his chest. He pulled me into a huddled position on the ground with him, one where I ended up sitting on his bent thighs with his arms wrapped around my body.

Despite our intimate position, I couldn't stop laughing.

The long grass that surrounded us itched, and I had an irrational fear of ghost crabs, but nothing could spoil this moment. Resting my head against Noah's shoulder, I tried to regain some composure but was surprised when I realized he too was laughing.

"You ran so fast," I muttered between breaths.

"I had to get you out of there. No one gets to see what's mine."

My laughter died, and I pulled back to better see his face. "Yours? Really?"

"Yes, Georgie, really. You're mine," he said definitely. He rested his forehead against mine, staring into my eyes. "You. Are. Mine. There's no going back from here."

In a heartbeat, our light mood turned serious. Something completely different took over and started crackling through the air, almost like the atmosphere had become electrically charged between us. I was now hyperaware of the way I was sitting, legs spread, on his thighs. He seemed conscious of this, too. His blunt fingernails dug into my hips and a slow, almost animalistic groan left his throat. My body reacted instantly to this change in him. Like he was a tiger ready to pounce and I was his prey, waiting eagerly to be eaten. *Holy shit, Noah!* My skin tingled, my nipples pricked, and the muscles low in my belly clenched—every ounce of my being became desperate for whatever was about to happen next.

He swore and tugged my body closer to his, kissing me hard. He'd never been rough with me before but for the briefest of moments he was a far cry away from gentle. His tongue dipped into my mouth, claiming and taking, before retreating. He withdrew from our kiss and took his t-shirt from the pile of clothes I still held in my arms, tugging it quickly over my head, while I carelessly dropped the rest of the clothes to the sand.

For a moment I thought he was doing this to get me dressed, so that we could go back to my house or something, but instead I think he only meant to cover my back from the prickly grass. Because in the next second, he gently pushed me down and showed me exactly what it meant to be his.

NOAH

Slow down, Noah, slow the hell down, I screamed inside my head.

I didn't listen to myself.

Sex on the beach wasn't as romantic as it sounded. I knew this from experience. Mostly—rather than a good time—both parties ended up with a lot of sand in places they didn't want. And those white crabs, the ones that hid out in those holes in the sand, freaked the hell out of me. Some of them had to be lurking in the tall grass that surrounded our hideout. But that became the least of my worries—because Georgie's cheeks were flushed, her eyes wide, and her body deliciously naked, screaming to be taken.

So, what the fuck else was I supposed to do?

I pulled my larger shirt down over her small body because I wasn't about to let anyone else lay their eyes on her perfect tits. So far I doubted anyone had seen anything, but I needed to keep it that way. Plus...sand was a bitch. What I really needed was a giant towel but my shirt would have to do.

With one hand on her shoulder and the other behind the small of her back, I gently guided her so she'd lay down for me. She did. So trusting, so easygoing, so much the opposite of me. It made me wonder—was it me who brought out her carefree side or was it just her?

"Noah," she half-moaned half-pleaded as some of her long hair tangled with the grass.

Yanking the rubber band from my own hair, I helped her become better situated and then used my palm to press the grass flat around her. Once she was comfortable, it occurred to me that this little spot of ours was pretty perfect. The tall grass hid us well, the morning breeze off the ocean was just chilly enough to send beautiful patches of goosebumps across Georgie's bare legs and stomach, and the roaring sound of the waves drowned out everything else.

Although…it didn't hurt that I had one hell of a gorgeous view.

When we sat down among the grass, Georgie sat with her legs spread against my knees. And when she'd laid backward and her little plump ass had remained on my knees, my view only became better. Her uncomfortableness with her hair had distracted me for a small second, but now that I'd helped her fix that, I took a moment to fully appreciate what a beautiful girl she was. Because, damn, I was one lucky son of a bitch.

Hard enough to pound nails, my dick throbbed and had grown painful. I wanted so badly to ease forward and slip inside her. Her swollen pink folds were wet and ready, and paired with the way her eyes kept raking over me, watching me—I knew she wanted me to fuck her. Desperately. I'd never felt such a rush of emotions coursing through my veins in my entire life. I ran my hands up and down her thighs, taking in the feel of her soft skin, careful *not* to touch where I wanted to most, stuck in my own personal hell.

Dammit. You know, I really *had* tried. I'd tried my fucking damnedest to go slow with her from the start. I think, whether I wanted to admit it to myself or not, I'd known I wanted more with her ever since that first night we'd slept in the same bed together. But I was also terrified. I'd had a few relationships in the past, some better than others, but never before had I felt something so heart-pounding, so irrational, and so perfect in my life. It scared the shit out of me to feel all of this. Because what if I let her in and then lost her? What if *I* wasn't enough to take away her pain? What if one day she tried to take her own life again? Where would that leave me? Alone. That was where. And I'd already had enough *alone* to last me a lifetime.

"Noah, please," she said, breaking me away from my thoughts. Her voice was rough and a little shaky. "I want this. I want *you*. If you're trying to tease me or something, then you've already succeeded at that."

Something deep inside me snapped. I was a man, and I only had so much control. If this girl wanted me then she could have me—all of me. My heart was beating like mad as my hands tightened under her thighs, lifting her closer to me. I pressed the head of my cock against her pretty entrance and let myself penetrate her slightly.

"Yes," she purred, moving her arms to rest above her head. "God, yes, Noah."

Shit. If she kept making sexy little noises then I was going to come before I even made it all the way in. Her blue eyes settled on mine. They were intense, but trusting, and the only thing I focused on as I pressed in deeper.

Holy Mother of Fuck. She was tight. *Too* very tight. But I felt no barrier so I knew she wasn't a virgin. That was probably something I should have considered earlier but hadn't. Her 'do-me-please-do-me-Noah' eyes hadn't led me to believe she was inexperienced, but as I struggled a little to get inside her, I realized she couldn't have done this more than once or twice before. I selfishly loved the thought of that. Because…this was some kind of heaven that I was sinking into. From now until forever, I only wanted her to know what *I* felt like inside her.

At the thought of anyone else *ever* getting to touch her, a growl slipped from my throat. That wouldn't be happening. I'd make damn certain of it. I pushed the rest of the way inside her. Once there, even though my body was roaring at me to move, I found that I desperately needed to kiss her. I needed to know she was okay, and I suppose, give her the chance to shove me away if she needed it.

So I bent over, kissing her plump lips, tasting her and reminding her that it was me who was buried deep inside her. She didn't shove me anywhere and instead met my kiss equally. Just as my hips were barely able to stay still a second longer, she whispered, "Don't you dare be gentle with me, Noah. You're sweet as hell, but I don't need sweet right now."

I swallowed hard. She said those words as if she'd read my concerns straight out of my mind. I was on the verge of falling off a very steep cliff. She knew it too and opened her legs wider against me. And then something astonishing happened. I gave up my worrying, all my inhibitions, and I completely let go.

I inched up the t-shirt that covered her chest, still holding her ass off the sand, and exposed more of her to me. I palmed the full weight of one those gorgeous tits, my thumb tracing lightly over her tight, pink nipple. Then I slid out of her and was far from gentle as I slammed back inside her.

We both cried out. So I did it again.

With each hard thrust her beautiful tits bounced, and it was the best sight in the world. I pulled her ass higher off the ground, desperate to be buried even deeper, rolling my hips before finding a nice, even rhythm. It was so damn sweet. *She* was so damn sweet.

She started chanting my name, softly at first, but then louder and louder with each thrust, until my name turned into a rough, anxious plea. It was the best fucking of my life. But I'd grown too sensitive, too fast. Feeling everything she had to give had me ready to burst.

Shit. I couldn't let myself go until she did.

"Dammit, Georgie," I growled.

Taking hold of one of her hands, I yanked her up, off the ground and toward me. Now she was practically riding me, her weight resting on my thighs. Gripping her ass, I held her and helped her bounce, hard and fast, up and down my length. Gravity on my side, I was able to thrust even deeper than before. That shirt of mine was still pushed up and over her gorgeous tits. Her hard little nipples brushed against my chest with each movement, driving me wild. Clutching my shoulders for support, her panting changed into satisfied little yelps. Her head dropped against my shoulder, while her body melted into me.

I loved how she let me move her.

However.

I.

Damn.

Well.

Pleased.

And then suddenly, as if I wasn't about to combust already, she slipped her arm down between us. "Fuck, no, sweetheart," I gasped and moved her hand to the side so mine could take its place.

I ran my thumb in small circles over her little sweet spot. She was soaking wet, so slick that my touch easily glided against her. She cried out, so responsive, and so loud that we were probably both about to get arrested. I didn't give a fuck. Because, from the desperate look in her eyes, I knew she was extremely close.

"Come for me," I bit out. "Please. Georgie. Sweetheart. Now. I need to feel it. Now—"

And she came. Her nails dug into my back as she buried her face into my neck, the muffled cries of my name lost against my skin. Her tight walls squeezed against me, over and over. I continued pumping into her hard and fast, never slowing, giving her all of me without holding back.

But I couldn't last another second. I thrust deeply into her one final time before I followed her over that mind-shattering edge. I hadn't worn a condom—like the biggest, stupidest idiot ever—and in my moment of ecstasy, I exploded inside her.

For a man, coming was the reward of all rewards. No other high on the planet could compare. But coming inside Georgina...fucking nirvana. And I knew I'd never be the same after this.

Tremors rocked through me and I think I told her something, but I can't be certain. Utterly spent, my body stilled against hers. Slowly blood started to return to my brain. And the moment that I'd regained a little cognitive functioning, I eased her back down onto the sand and pulled out. Because I knew that if I didn't move away immediately then I'd become hard once more and would have to have her again. Immediately. I collapsed beside her. My breathing was so rapid that it felt like I'd ran a marathon.

Sweet bliss didn't last forever. A few moments of contentment was all I was granted and then shame settled. I couldn't believe how quickly all that had happened. I'd acted like some horny, crazed, overzealous teenager. Having sex. Outside. With no condom. In the damn sand!

I sighed, running my hands through my hair and then dropping them back at my sides. *Jesus Christ, Noah! How could I be so careless?* I felt like something amazing was happening between us. Something that should be cherished and never rushed. Something that made me want to crawl out of my safe little hole—like one of those damn white, ghost crabs—and finally start fully living my life. And I felt like a jackass for how quickly I'd rushed to have sex with her.

Because that wasn't what this was about. Not hardly.

Fear washed over me next. If I just ruined everything with Georgie then I wasn't sure how I'd ever recover. I was about to apologize, and possibly start groveling, when her small hand slipped into mine. She let out a sexy little laugh—one that hit me like giant bowling ball, square in the middle of my chest.

"What's so funny?" I choked out.

"Nothing," she said softly. "Everything… You."

"Me?"

"Yes. You're so unexpected and fun, still kind of weird, but in a good way, and I'm having a really great time hanging out with you. Seriously, Noah. You're worth living for."

Holy shit. The air left my lungs. I couldn't believe she'd said that.

I sat up, taking in the sight of her, and was suddenly unable to wipe a big-ass grin off my face—because Georgie had a seriously satisfied look on her face. I'd just had wild caveman sex with her, and I was relieved to find that she seemed to be perfectly okay with that.

My mind was made up—she *was* mine. Or at least, I was hers. And I was going to prove myself worthy of this girl. "I'm having fun hanging out with you too," I said. "If 'hanging out' is what you want to call it. But it's not me. It's all you. You're the one bringing me to life."

Her cheeks flushed. "Thanks, Noah," she whispered. "I think."

I couldn't help myself; I bent over and kissed her. My lips moved slowly against hers, savoring. Then I broke away because I needed to get her off this beach before we actually did get arrested. "I need you dressed and safe at home. Someone might have heard us."

"Was I loud?"

Loud was an understatement. "Only a little," I lied.

Finding her black panties from our mixed pile of clothes, I helped her place each foot through the leg holes. Then I inched the sheer material over her calves and up her thighs—doing my very best to ignore how perfect she looked messed up from all my…relentlessness. A little *relentlessness* dripped in a liquid path down the inside of her thigh. And, *fuck me*, I couldn't help myself when my finger trailed over the spot, pushing my semen back up toward where it belonged, and spreading it across her wetness. I pushed one finger inside her. Then stopped myself.

Shit. Having sex with her once only made me want her more. Usually sex worked the opposite way, cured you of your desire for that other person, but not with her. She was an exception to every rule. I already knew that though, and as I pulled away from her, our eyes connecting briefly, and I whispered, "Again. But not now." It was a promise and a threat.

She sat up and pulled her cotton shorts on next, while I stood to put on my pajama pants. We were a both bit sandy, but if Georgie minded, she didn't say anything.

She was smiling and my heart was swelling as we walked hand-in-hand, along the (thankfully deserted) beach, back toward her house. We weren't talking, but we didn't need to. Then it occurred to me that I had butterflies in my stomach. I'd already seen her naked. Didn't butterflies typically happen *before* that sort of thing? They were churning and gut-clenching—a wonderful kind of high.

We reached her back door, the one at ground level. I glanced toward the neighbor's house, but everything seemed quiet in that direction. So I focused only on Georgie. I hated that I had to leave her now.

"I can't come inside with you. I want to. But can't. I'd actually really like to tell your parents about us. Rose too. Anyone who fucking wants to hear it." Great, I wasn't very smooth at baring my soul, but she needed to know all this. "If we tell your parents, then the spending the night thing is probably going to have to stop. I'm not ready for that to stop."

"Me neither," she said, looking down at my two hands that were clutching one of hers.

"I've got to go find Rhett too," I explained. Though she probably didn't need such a thorough explanation. And yet, all of it kept slipping out of my mouth anyway. *Was I nervous…still…even after everything that had just happened?* I kept rambling. "Last night, I saw that girl he's been searching everywhere for—his mystery girl. I spoke with her and she basically told me she wants nothing to do with him. He's not going to take that well. Anyway…I parked a few houses down last night."

"Okay," she simply said. "If I don't see you before tonight, then I'll see you in bed. Right?"

"Yes." But she was going to see me before that.

She stood on her tiptoes, pressed a quick kiss to my lips, and then opened the door to her house. "Bye, Noah," she whispered over her shoulder. "Good luck with Rhett and… Best. Morning. Ever." Then she disappeared inside.

Shit. *What the hell was this girl doing to me?*

chapter 16

GEORGINA

I shut the door and sagged against it, letting a hiss of air flow through my teeth. I had it *bad* for this man. Seriously, bad. Like can't-see-straight, can't-function-properly, can't-feel-my-toes, don't-even-care bad.

Damn. A shirtless image of Noah—the hard lines of his tight, tanned stomach, the little beads of sweat, the trail of dark hair that started at his belly button and led straight down, and the powerful, life-changing sight of *all of him* buried deep inside me, pumping hard and sure. These images were stuck in my mind and kept playing on repeat. He hadn't held back for a single second while we were together, exactly liked I'd wanted, and a rougher, wilder Noah had emerged. I kind of knew that rougher side was there all along, but I never could have prepared my body for it.

Damn. Just thinking about it had me tingling all over again. I needed someone to dump ice down my pants. And then unexpectedly a small knock sounded behind me. I scrambled to my feet, my knees a little weak and wobbly, confused but ecstatic at who might be on the other side. Opening the door, my eyes met Noah's.

My breathing was a mess. "What are you doing back so soon?"

He stared at me for several long seconds. Finally he spoke. "Are you okay? Your cheeks are red."

My face burned. "I'm fine."

"You don't look fine," he said and smiled for a brief second like he knew exactly what was wrong with me. Then his hand met the small of my waist. He slowly and forcefully pushed, walking me backward inside my house. His lips were inches from mine, his jaw tense, and his pupils dilated. "I forgot a few things," he said in a low voice. "My keys. My wallet. My shoes. Possibly my damn mind."

Suddenly he lifted me up. My legs locked automatically around his waist and my mouth crashed down on his. The two little words he'd whispered as he came inside me replayed in my head. *Only you.* I wasn't sure if Noah and I made much sense logically, but that was quickly becoming one of my favorite things about us. I loved the lack of pressure I felt with him, and how quickly one little kiss could make me lose all inhibitions. I'd never experienced anything like this, even with Logan. It was scary and liberating at the same time.

"Noah," I whispered, breaking my lips from his.

"I know," he answered, setting me down. "I know. I can't lose control here. You make that pretty close to impossible. C'mon." He tugged on my hand. I followed him back to the guest bedroom where he slipped on his shoes and pocketed all his other belongings. Then we walked back to the door.

"Goodbye again," he whispered, brushing a few loose strands of my hair behind my ear and pressing one final kiss to my forehead. "You're driving me insane."

"I'm sorry," I muttered but wasn't sorry at all.

"It's a good kind of insane."

Then he slipped out the door, disappearing once more, leaving me with smile on my face. One I had a feeling I'd be wearing all freaking day long.

* * *

"Georgina, honey," Mom called.

Rose and I were watching her favorite reality TV family...again. "So what happened with Khloe's husband? They seemed so in love."

"He's too jealous," Rose said, shaking her little head at me. "Just shut up and watch. It's not *that* hard to follow. Khloe and her husband are getting a divorce now. How come you don't already know this? Everybody knows this."

I hated to admit it, but I was starting to get sucked into Rose's shows. Drama. Drama. Drama. On the plus side, her shows made me feel relatively normal. And Khloe was pretty freaking hilarious to watch.

"Georgina," Mom said, moving to stand in front of the TV.

Rose and I both groaned.

She propped her hands on her hips. "Oh no. You aren't missing anything. This stuff is going to rot your brains. Anyway, I need to go meet your dad with some papers. And we were thinking about staying out and having dinner after. It's been a very long time since we've done anything just the two of us. If I leave you with some money for pizza, would you mind watching Rose tonight? I know it's your night off, but would that be okay?"

"What am I?" Rose complained. "Chopped liver. Nobody asks if anything is okay with me."

My mom's eyes pleaded with mine. Her dark hair was a little frizzy and falling from the knot she had twisted it into behind her head. Maybe she needed a break or something—desperately—because she looked like she could snap at any moment. Which, actually, seemed more like the Mom I remembered from before my 'incident' than the careful version of herself that she'd become lately.

"I'll watch her," I said. "We can watch episodes of the Kardashians all night."

"Ugh," Rose groaned, slapping her hands on her thighs. "I'll be the one watching *her.*"

From Mom's pocket, her cell phone rang. She jumped at the sound. "That's your dad. Please, guys, stop arguing. I guess I can call Mrs. Bailey to come over and babysit."

"Not Mrs. Bailey," Rose gasped. "Never mind. Georgina can watch me."

Mom's eyes were still pleading—maybe only with herself. Was she nervous to leave me alone at the house? I guess she had every right to be. "I'm fine," I said. "Really. I won't do anything dumb while you're gone. So stop worrying and have a good night with Dad."

"I know," she whispered, water pooling in her eyes. "You've been so much happier over the past week; happier than you've been in over a year. I've noticed and frankly, I'm relieved. So…I will leave you some money on the counter for pizza." She smiled. "And you girls have a good night."

"Whatever," Rose mumbled.

"Bye, Mom," I said, ignoring the tears that were trying to pool behind my eyes.

When I'd taken the knife to my arms I'd thought only of myself and never of the effect my actions would have on my family. I hadn't even thought of the additional pain I would cause each of them. Correction. The additional pain I was *still* causing each of them. That awareness sat like a giant boulder on my chest.

I *had* to make everything right.

Imagine if Rose, instead of having one dead sibling, now had *two*. I ached, like never before, for my sister. I wanted to find a way to lessen any pain she might be experiencing. No kid should ever have to go through all this crap.

The moment Mom left and it was just the two of us, the first words that slipped from my mouth were, "I'm sorry."

Rose stared straight ahead at the television.

"When I tried to kill myself, I wasn't thinking about anyone but me. That was, and will probably always be, the biggest mistake of my life." Tears decided to burst free from my eyes, leaking down my cheeks. Rose, however, was much tougher than me. She sat, still staring at the screen, completely unaffected. "I can't undo my mistake. But I can promise you that I won't ever do it again. I know you must be hurting inside. And I'm so sorry that I've added to that pain, Rosie. I felt so alone when I tried to kill myself, but maybe if we could all just hurt together then none of us would have to go through this alone."

I groaned, burying my face in my hands. I wasn't even making any sense. Rose was wicked smart, and she had to think I was acting totally pathetic right about now.

But then suddenly I uncovered my eyes…because two skinny arms had wrapped around my waist, squeezing me as tight as possible.

"You're not alone, Georgie," Rose whispered, her little voice cracking as she tried to comfort *me*. I was the older one; that meant I should be the one doing the comforting. Not the other way around.

"You aren't alone either," I whispered, returning her embrace.

We sat together, hugging for a very long time. Eventually, after counting one hundred and fifty-two of my breaths, I calmed down and the tears dried. Then we let go of each other and both settled back on the couch.

"Dammit," Rose said, her tone half-joking. "You made me miss that entire episode!"

"Don't swear," I warned in a hollow threat.

"Whatever. Mom isn't here."

I laughed. "Fine. You can swear but only when it's just the two of us."

She smiled mischievously. *Oh, no. What had I unleashed?* This girl was trouble waiting to happen. "Can we take Mom's twenty bucks and go out to eat? Please. Pretty please. I've got some money. I'll pay the difference if it costs extra."

We'd never gone out to eat before—just the two of us. And suddenly I really wanted to. I needed her to think of me as that *cool big sister* again.

I agreed.

Then we hurried for the car, even though it was barely past four in the afternoon, and drove the short distance to the Blue Pelican. *Jeez.* The Blue Pelican was about the last place I wanted to go, but Rose demanded crab legs, and I felt a wonderful surge of energy coursing through my veins. It was *me* who had Noah Clark crawling into *my* bed every night. Those were some serious bragging rights. And now that I'd made up my mind about my suicide attempt, knowing wholeheartedly that it had been a mistake, I felt like I could take on whatever the world had to throw at me.

Sonya Fletcher couldn't deter me. No one could.

I parked. Rose and I walked in through the familiar painted blue doors, a giant marlin in a net hanging ridiculously from the ceiling. The hostess recognized me, made small talk, and then led us toward a booth in the back of the dimly lit restaurant. The place was already packed since many of the tourists liked to eat dinner early to avoid the crowds and take a break from the sun.

"I feel like we're on a date," Rose said, in awe. "This table is kind of high. Would you be embarrassed if I asked for a booster seat?"

It took me a couple seconds, but it occurred to me she was only joking and I burst out laughing. "You're something else, Rose." And then, as we were waiting for the server to come introduce herself before we hit the buffet, I decided I wanted to tell Rose everything about Noah. I found I needed to tell someone, anyone, desperately.

"I have something to share, and you can't tell Mom," I started.

Those were the magic words. She dropped her kids menu and stared at me with the most eager eyes. "I can keep a secret. I promise."

Hoping I wouldn't regret telling her this, I took a breath and let the words slip out. "I think I'm in love with Noah Clark."

She stared at me for several long seconds, then finally spoke. "You're shitting me."

"Don't curse," I groaned.

"Whatever. Don't change the subject. So, you *think* you love him or you *know* you love him?"

Wow. She was more quizzical than one of my therapists. "Know," I whispered, swallowing hard. I *did* love him. Wildly and without doubt. It was impossible not to fall, crashing and burning, head-over-heels for a man like Noah.

"Then you should know..." Rose said, her face turning rather pale. "Noah is here right now. Over there." She pointed.

Holy shit. I glanced over my shoulder and sure enough—there was Noah. Except he wasn't alone. He sat in a booth, a gorgeous blonde in the seat across from him. "What the hell?" I said under my breath, doing a double take. No, my eyes weren't lying to me. It was definitely *my* Noah. "How long has he been over there?" I asked Rose.

"The whole time," she answered. "I didn't know you liked him or even cared about him, or I would have pointed him out sooner. I wanted to go say hi when we came in, but I thought since he was on a date, it would be rude to interrupt."

My heart crashed to the floor and splintered into a million little pieces. He *was* on a date with someone else. We'd never officially been on a date. Instead he'd screwed me in the sand. After this morning, this was the last thing I ever expected.

Stupid.

I was beyond stupid.

I inched further into the booth. He obviously hadn't seen me. *But did that even matter?* "We need to leave. Now," I muttered to Rose. The smell of crab legs wafting through the air had my stomach churning. And the worst part of all—I was a little sore. Before this morning, it had been ages since I'd last had sex, even sex with Logan had never been anything like it was with Noah, and I squeezed my legs together trying to erase the reminder of where he'd been. Not to mention, I still was wearing his damn t-shirt. I had it tied on the side, so it didn't look completely ridiculous, but I'd kept it on since I'd wanted to keep a piece of him close to me all day. Now it felt so itchy against my skin that I nearly was willing to rip it off right then and there.

Rose stretched her hand across the table and locked it in mine. "Maybe she's his friend." *Jeez,* she was trying to comfort me *again*.

"No, Rose," I whispered. "Men don't have friends that look like that girl."

Seriously, the girl looked like she'd stepped from the pages of a Victoria Secret catalog. I'd hate to see her in a swimsuit. A southern beauty. Her blond hair was voluminous, wavy, and perfect, and she had an innocence about her I could tell wasn't real but men would eat up...damn. I knew I was pretty, but not like her. She was a girl's worst freaking nightmare. I *had* to stop staring at them, deep in conversation—because I was seconds away from crying.

"Ohmigod," Sonya suddenly said, appearing out of nowhere. *Perfect luck.* It seemed our server was going to be Sonya. Of all people, of all times, Sonya. "Did ya'll come in here just to visit me?" she asked sweetly.

"No," Rose automatically answered.

"Oh," Sonya said, turning to glance in Noah's direction. "He's why you're here, isn't he? Talking to *her*. Can you believe how much she's changed?"

"Who is she?" I asked, dumbfounded.

"Sydney Michaels. From our grade. Crazy, huh?"

Sydney Michaels was a quiet, studious girl with light brown hair, glasses, and average looks. We'd had a couple classes together over the years but had never spoken. The girl sitting across from Noah wasn't Sydney. At least, not the Sydney I remembered. *What the hell happened to her?*

"She changed about the time...well...when you left school," Sonya said, answering my unspoken question. "Maybe your brush with death inspired her or something. Forced the girl out of her shell. She dyed her hair, got contacts, put on some makeup, and actually started to be friendly. Weird, huh? And she turned into a slut too. She's on break. She's got like fifteen minutes left, but do you want me to go tell her to get back to work?"

"She works here?"

"Yeah. Started a couple weeks ago."

So, Noah was here visiting her on her break. Fantastic. Just effing fantastic. I gathered up my purse. "I don't want you to tell her anything. I have nothing to say to either one of them. But will you let Rose and me sneak out through the back?"

"Sure, babe." She gave me a small smile, making me miss the girl she used to be—the girl I'd grown up with. Rose and I followed Sonya out through the kitchen. My heart was in my shoes. Noah had used his shyness and his vulnerability to fool me straight into bed. And I was the young, naive, stupid girl who'd fallen for his act. Hook. Line. And sinker.

But as we followed Sonya, a silver lining emerged. My ex-friend was being helpful and nice. Maybe, like Rose, the rift between us was all my doing. *If I apologized to Sonya could I start to mend everything that was broken between us?*

"I'll make sure she gets the shitty side-work when her shift is over tonight," Sonya offered, hesitating as she let us out the back door.

"Thanks," I muttered, grabbing Rose's hand. "And, Sonya, please call me sometime. There's stuff we need to talk about. Stuff that probably should be said."

She nodded, her eyes on the door rather than mine. "You know Logan and I are sort of seeing each other? We were out together when you saw us at Chancy's."

Logan had mentioned that he and Sonya were hanging out some. I hadn't considered the possibility that that meant they were dating. But as Sonya's words sank in, I found I didn't really care all that much. They could date each other if they wanted to. I wouldn't get in their way. "Still call me," I added.

Rose and I left the restaurant, heading home. The sky had turned grey and ominous, which matched my mood perfectly. "Sorry our dinner date was ruined," I told her on the drive. So much for me being the *cool big sister*. Sneaking out through the back of the Blue Pelican had felt like the ultimate walk of shame, and I was still splintering inside. I tried to keep calm—for Rose's sake.

"That's okay," Rose said, but I heard a trace of disappointment in her voice. Maybe I shouldn't have left the restaurant. Maybe I should have confronted Noah head on, but I hadn't wanted to do it while wearing his t-shirt.

"I need to go home and change. Then we can figure out something else to do tonight."

"You still want to do something with me?" she asked eagerly.

"Of course, Rosie." I turned the steering wheel, pulling down our street. "Noah's just a boy. I won't let him spoil our evening."

Too bad that *boy* happened to be waiting at my house. In his damn leather jacket again, leaning against his damn motorcycle, with damn flowers in his hand, looking like something out of a dream. *Why flowers? And how the heck had he beat us home?* "Stay in the car for a minute," I told Rose as we pulled up to the house. I was beyond shocked to find him there, and it wasn't a good kind of shocked. "This is going to get ugly."

Keep breathing, dammit, I thought just as the sky opened up and a light rain started.

chapter **17:**

NOAH

There she was. A calmness settled over me, one that I hadn't felt since morning. It had been a shitty day. I never should have left her earlier, because each and every single second since I last saw her had been worse than the one before it.

It started at the pharmacy. I spent a full hour there, debating over whether or not I should buy her a damn morning-after pill or Plan-B or whatever you want to call it. I paced the aisles, shirtless, because I'd left my shirt with Georgie, Googling every possible side-effect on my phone. Finally, I decided that I couldn't show up at her house with the pill. What kind of asshole would that make me? I needed to talk to her first. I would have called her then and there but, like a fool, I didn't even have her phone number. *God, I was the worst boyfriend ever. Fuck. Was I her boyfriend?*

In the end, all I bought was a box of condoms, avoided some weird looks from the clerk who'd seen me pacing for an hour, and headed home. On my way, I had the overwhelming urge to buy the girl flowers. Georgia was the type who deserved flowers, not condoms and pills. I'd never bought a woman flowers before. Well, technically, that wasn't true. I had already bought them for Georgie once before—after her suicide attempt and while she was still in the hospital. I hadn't written my name on the card, so I was sure she never knew they were from me, but buying them had felt like something I'd needed to do at the time. And, again, I had the urge to buy her flowers. So I made a mental note to do that later.

Once home, I showered and did my normal cleaning routine. Mostly, I was killing time, waiting on Rhett to get home. He must have stayed out somewhere, because he wasn't in his room and he wasn't answering his cell. Maybe he'd spent the night with one of his usual fuck buddies, meaning he was over his infatuation with his mystery girl. Good. Because I was confident this girl, the one I'd spoken with at The Swing the other night, had been the same girl from Ben's funeral.

I had a theory on why she'd been crying her eyes out too. Because you didn't cry like that unless you knew the person who'd died and knew them well. So now, more than ever, I wanted to know who the hell Rhett's mystery girl was. What was her link to Ben? Whether I was figuring it out for Georgie or Ellie or the whole Turner family, I wasn't sure. But they were my family too, and I needed to solve this small mystery for them. I couldn't wait around all day for Rhett.

So, I followed my only lead—her jackass brother, Three Lip Rings, and went to the closest tattoo parlor. Mystery Blonde never said her own name, but she'd mentioned her brother's name. John. The guy had more ink than bare skin, and it was the only spot I could think to look.

I walked into the place, and lo and behold, there he was. Working.

"Can I help—" Lip Ring John started to say as he glanced up from the woman he was tattooing. He noticed it was me, and his eyes automatically narrowed. "Unless you're here to get some ink then get your ass out of my shop," he said, venom dripping in his voice. Three other guys glanced up from their stations, all giving me equally dirty looks.

You've got to be shitting me.

Breathing in deep, I tried to remain calm. I wasn't a 'people person.' Talking with strangers was a weakness of mine. So talking with assholes...well, that triggered a whole different side of my personality. I had traces of my Uncle Joe's temper buried deep inside me, and I didn't like putting myself in situations where that side might surface.

"I need to speak with your sister," I said, keeping an even voice.

"Get in line, pal. She ain't talking with your dickhead friend, and she ain't gonna be talking with you. So both of you get your sorry asses out of her life."

Every bone in my body wanted to turn around and simply leave, but I forced myself to stay put. "I'm not here for Rhett. I'm here for my girlfriend." The lie slipped from my tongue so easily that it felt real. Maybe it was real. "Her name is Georgina Turner. Ben Turner was her brother. Does that name mean anything to you?"

"Yes," he uttered, and it was like a flip switched. His guard-dog attitude dropped. "It means something."

Wow. Ben must have known this guy too. My stomach turned. *How many secrets did this kid keep?* "Can you please tell me where I can find your sister? I'd like to talk to her about Ben. Not Rhett."

His eyes went back to the woman before him. He started his ink gun again, pressing it to her already sunburned skin, and she winced a little at the pain. I thought for a moment John was going to ignore me, but then he started talking as he worked.

"Sydney's got herself a waitressing job over at that all-you-eat crab place. The fancy one with the big fish on the ceiling. She's a good girl. She'll tell you whatever you want to know about Ben. You get your answers and then you leave my sister the hell alone. She's already been through enough this year."

That was all he said. But that was all I needed to know. The mystery girl had a name. Sydney. And she worked at the Blue Pelican. I'd never been there before, kind of fancy for my blood too, but the big fish on the ceiling had its own reputation. So I knew exactly where to go. I left John's shop, making a pit-stop at the florist, and headed to the Blue Pelican next.

* * *

"What are you? Houdini?" Georgie huffed, slamming her car door as she stepped out onto the driveway. She wore my white t-shirt from this morning—the only thing she'd had on while I'd been buried deep inside her. Damn. I thoroughly enjoyed seeing her in my shirt. It conjured up *very* good memories. Memories I had every intention of repeating as soon as possible. I adjusted my pants, because damn, the girl had me instantly hard.

I cleared my throat. "Houdini? Like the magician?"

Wait. Her eyes were rimmed in red. Shit. Something was off.

"Yes, like the magician." She rushed around the car, opening the passenger door. Rose popped out. I'd been too distracted that I hadn't noticed she had Rose with her. I watched as Georgie whispered something to the girl and ushered her toward the house. They both hurried past me like I wasn't there. *What the hell?*

"Georgie, wait," I rushed after them, still clutching the damn flowers in my hand. It had started to rain, and I hoped that was the reason both girls were in a hurry, but something told me it wasn't the rain. Rose fumbled with the key, ignoring me when she normally was always thrilled to see me. I caught Georgie's arm because she hadn't even made fucking eye contact with me. Her face was splotchy red, as if she'd been crying or was seconds away from crying. I didn't know her well enough yet to know which.

"What's going on?" I whispered. "If someone did *anything* to you, so much as looked at you funny, then I will fucking end them. Tell me what happened. Why are you upset?"

She glanced up, glaring at me. Whatever pain she felt…it ricocheted through me. Because her blue eyes, the color magnified by the red that lined them, were devastating. "You're what happened," she muttered.

The breath left my lungs. I dropped my hold on her arm, stunned, and frankly, crushed. Rose managed to unlock the door and both girls disappeared inside. It felt like someone had cut my knees out from under me. I stood, staring at the door for a moment, shell-shocked, until it occurred to me that I had a key and could follow her inside. I didn't have a damn clue as to what I did wrong, but whatever I did, I would fix it.

I unlocked the door and found Georgie sitting on the floor. Rose had her arms wrapped around her. Like if she could squeeze her sister tight enough then she could squeeze away all her pain. I knew that feeling. I'd lived through it once before—when I'd waited for the paramedics to arrive. I didn't get it. The Georgie I knew was such a strong person. Why would she ever let anything, including me, affect her like this?

I dropped on the floor beside them. "Please…" My voice cracked, and I sure as fuck wasn't ever one to become emotional. "Tell me what I did. I need to know so I can fix it. Please, Georgie. What happened?"

She didn't answer me or even look at me. But Rose did. "We saw you with your girlfriend and you were on a date," she said, sassing me.

Did she mean Sydney? At the Blue Pelican? Not ten minutes ago? I guess the Houdini reference made sense now. We must have been there at the same time, and Georgie must have automatically assumed the worst. I blew out a breath of relief, glad she didn't hate me for something more than this simple misunderstanding. "That wasn't a date," I started. "I didn't even order a glass of water. I only stopped there to speak with Sydney. She's the girl Rhett's been searching for."

"You weren't on a date with her?" Georgie asked, her eyes still avoiding mine.

"Of course not. She means nothing to me. Look at me, Georgie, please."

She did. And *holy shit* those eyes of hers were fierce. She wasn't crying at all. She was only pissed off. "I want to believe you, Noah. But I've been hurt before. Just like this. Why would you be any different? You were so deep in conversation with her that you didn't even notice Rose and me come into the restaurant. We were in a booth only twenty feet away from you. And all I could think was—what if you got all you wanted from me this morning and we were over?"

Fuck that.

The sharpness and the edge in her eyes scared the shit out of me. She had the power to break me. "This morning was the tip of the iceberg for us," I told her firmly. "Nothing is over. You mean *everything* to me, and that's not something I'd let slip away over such a silly misunderstanding like this. Sydney and I were deep in conversation only because we were talking about your brother. She was in love with Ben. She'd always been in love with him. Even when he didn't know she existed in high school, she'd loved him. Then I guess whenever Ben took classes at the community college—the ones he took so he could graduate early—she'd had classes with him. They became friends. I don't know any more than that. I don't know why she randomly slept with Rhett and I don't even care. Because none of that matters right this moment. Not now. Not when I need to ask you one very important question?"

"What?" Most of her anger had mellowed but a trace of it was still there.

"Will *you* be my girlfriend?"

I'd never in all my life officially asked a girl this. I guess, when sex lasted more than one night, the term could be applied. But I didn't want any doubt—in my heart or in hers. Georgie had some serious trust issues to work through. Because when she saw me talking with Sydney she shouldn't have assumed the worst. But that didn't matter. I wanted her—issues and all. I had my own issues that needed work. Maybe we could figure these things out together.

"That's kind of random," she finally said in response to my question that still hung thick in the air between us. Not the answer I'd hoped for. Meanwhile, Rose had her mouth dropped open, gazing up at me while still holding her sister tight. I guess I was more entertaining than an episode of whatever reality show held her attention this week.

"I don't care if it's random," I said, interested in only what Georgie thought of me in this moment. "It's what I want. I think it might be what you want too."

She took a breath. "But I just accused you of something that was probably nothing."

"It *was* nothing." I ran my fingers through my hair, staring at her, still waiting for a damn answer. "But that doesn't change my mind. It only reconfirms what I already know. You're passionate as hell, and I love that about you."

A few more seconds ticked by and then she spoke again, still avoiding my question. "Well, I'm not sure if we even make sense together," she whispered, but it didn't sound like she believed her own words.

"It only has to make *sense* to us," I said softly. "And it makes perfect sense to me. Nothing has ever made more sense."

The smallest hint of a smile touched her lips. "Well, maybe you're a little too old for me?"

"Fu—Screw that," I huffed, trying my best to refrain from swearing any more than I already had in front of Rose. "I'm not a grandpa here."

A full smile filled her face. "I was only kidding. Don't get so defensive."

"Was that your last excuse?"

Georgie nodded, barely, but that nod meant everything to me.

Warmth burst through my chest. "Then tell me yes. Tell me you're mine. Because I need to hear you say the words."

"Yes, Noah," she said, confident and sure, surprising me by responding so quickly. "I'm yours. You didn't need to ask."

"Yes, I did."

It was a good thing Rose was in the room with us. Because if not, I would have covered her with my body and made love to her right there on the floor. And, once again, I wouldn't have had the chance to be gentle or slow. But dammit too, because I couldn't even kiss her—not with her little mini-me glued to her side. For as tiny as she was, Rose was protective as hell. It made me wish, for the first time in my life, that I had a brother or a sister. I'd never wanted one before, always thankful no one else had to experience my shitty upbringing, but the love this family shared was pretty special. I only hoped Georgie saw what I did.

I stood. Rose dropped her death-grip hold on her sister. And then the three of us went upstairs. I wasn't sure what we were going to do, but that didn't matter. This was the only place I wanted to be.

On the way up the steps, with Rose a few paces in front of us, I caught my girl's waist and pulled her back against my body, crushing the flowers that were still clutched in my hand against her. There was so much more I needed to say and most of it would have to wait until our time together tonight, but as Rose disappeared at the top of the stairs we had a small second alone and I took it. "I missed you," I whispered, because it was the truth, and because she needed to hear it. "You're all I've thought about—all day long. And I was counting down the seconds until I could get back here to you." I kissed her neck, breathing in the scent of her. She smelled like strawberries and the rain. I didn't want to let her go. "Please, don't doubt how crazy I am about you."

My grip around her waist tightened. I'd been so relentless with her out on the sand that I'd never given myself the chance to savor and explore.

My fingers trailed over her stomach, moved upward and brushing over her chest, as I kissed down her neck. She moaned and rested her head back against my shoulder. I itched with the need to take the full weight of one of her perfect tits in my hand once more. The beating rain outside matched the rhythm of my heart, but now wasn't the time to explore.

Reluctantly, I removed my body from her body.

She turned to around to look at me. Our eyes were level. "Why the flowers?"

I'd forgotten that I still held the thick stems in my hand. Sunflowers—slightly mangled and droopy now. They weren't good enough for her anymore—having survived the heat while I spoke with Sydney, the drive on my bike over here, and the last few minutes being clutched so tightly while Georgie put me through hell—but I handed them over to her anyway. I knew nothing about flowers, but I'd tried my best to pick something that fit her, and sunflowers were both strong and beautiful. "I wanted to get you something," I explained. It was the best explanation I could come up with. "My conscious keeps yelling at me to slow down, and maybe I should try to listen to myself, but I don't fucking care. Because when you know you know. And I *know* with you. So I got you flowers, and I'm probably going to do it again."

"Oh. Thank you," she muttered and for a fraction of a second, her thank-you felt like it was for more than the flowers. I'm not sure what *more* she might have meant, and I didn't ask. "I have to watch Rose tonight. Do you want to do that with me?"

"I have nowhere else I want to be, pretty girl, and that's why I'm here—to do whatever you're doing."

She nodded, saying nothing more, becoming a little quieter than usual. I was normally the quiet one, so her sudden shyness threw me off. We climbed the rest of the stairs, me doing my best to keep my hands off her, and joined Rose on the living room couch. Georgie used her mom's computer to order dinner for delivery and the three of us ended up staying in—watching a movie and eating pizza.

Rose had forgiven me. Because she was talkative and loud—back to her normal self and explaining way more than I ever needed to know on subjects that I couldn't care less about. Seriously. Someone needed to limit all the shit she watched on TV.

But something was still a little off with Georgie. She laughed at the movie, didn't resist me as I cuddled against her on the couch, and ate a few bites of pizza—but I could sense something wasn't right. It was such a slight change, so minuscule that even Rose didn't catch on, but I noticed it. And it made me realize how fucking brilliant she was at faking *everything* when she wanted to. The Georgie I'd come to know over the past few days hadn't been 'faking' anything—not for a single second, and I was pretty damn certain of that. But this Georgie...she wasn't quite *my* Georgie and I hated it.

"You're upset," I whispered against her ear when the movie had about thirty minutes left. I couldn't stand sitting still a second longer. "I can tell. I'm going to leave, go park my bike down the street, and then sneak into the guest room downstairs. Your parents will be home soon, but come get in bed with me as soon as you can. I'll be waiting."

chapter 18:

GEORGINA

Noah was an amazing man. I shouldn't have doubted him. He was surreal, handsome, thoughtful, and strangely interested in me. Why shouldn't monogamous be added to that list? He gave me those sunflowers, and they took me back in time to another memory of him. One I never knew belonged to him in the first place, and it made me realize how completely undeserving I was.

"Where should I put this one?" Mom asked, a small vase of sunflowers in her hand. Another flower arrangement had arrived. I had wealthy relatives out in Colorado and the things would not stop coming.

They were all too beautiful, and I felt only ugliness inside. I needed them gone. "Mom," I whined. I had a tube in my arm, was dressed in a paper-thin hospital gown, and was lying in a bed that wasn't the coffin I'd planned for yesterday. "Take them home, please."

Mom wore a purple shirt—one I hadn't seen her wear in many years. She'd been here since I arrived and Dad being Dad must have grabbed whatever out of her closet as a change of clothes. He didn't know any better. But somehow that purple shirt reminded me of my dead brother. I couldn't look at anyone or anything and not remember that he was gone.

"People send flowers because they love you," Mom explained as if I didn't already know that. "We all love you, Georgina. They're meant to cheer you up. Please, let me leave them here."

"No."

"How about just one?"

"Fine, whatever." I couldn't believe we were arguing about flowers. My brother was dead, and we were arguing about flowers.

She dropped a small white envelope onto the table beside me, adding it to a growing pile—one mini-size card always came with each arrangement, and I wasn't reading any of them. "I'm going down to the lobby to meet with the lady from The Cove. I'll talk to her first and then she'll come back here with me. We'll talk about options and decide if The Cove is the place that could help you. Please, just listen to the lady. Give her a chance."

Mom kept bringing up this place called 'The Cove.' A friend of a friend's daughter, or something random like that, went there, and they helped her deal with the death of her father. I didn't want to get over Ben. I didn't want to do anything. I only wanted the pain to disappear. I needed a miracle and for my brother to be alive—not a Shady-Acres, padded-wall mental hospital.

I sighed, too tired to argue. "Fine. I'll listen."

"Okay. I won't be gone long." Mom left and a nurse replaced her. She sat in a chair on the opposite end of the room, giving me my space, and not making conversation. I liked her. I liked when people stopped talking about what happened—stopped asking why. The 'why' was obvious, and yet, every single person who had been in here to visit me kept asking it. Mom. Dad. Ellie. But the problem with lack of conversation was…it gave me time to think about Ben and about all the people I'd let down yesterday. Jesus, help me. Because a giant part of me was still wishing yesterday's plan would have been successful.

Thanks a lot, Noah Clark, *I thought sarcastically.* It was his fault I still lived.

But, surprisingly enough, I wasn't mad at Noah. He saved me. I had a small memory of it—of him holding me, keeping me warm, and whispering something about 'not dying' in my ear. Mom explained how he'd been the one to find me and help me. I was alive because of him. And as much as I wanted to hate him for that, I couldn't. In fact, thinking about it had my throat clogging up and catching fire.

He'd fought for me. We barely knew each other, and he'd fought for me.

I rolled over onto my side and the little card that came with the sunflowers caught my eye. I'm not sure what made me do it, since I still wasn't about to read the rest of them, but I reached for it, wincing from the pain I felt in my arm. The pain medication had been forced on me yesterday, but I'd refused it today. So moving hurt.

I tore the little envelope. The inside card was plain white with extremely sloppy handwriting—handwriting that covered the front and back. And I had no clue who it was from. Not Logan. His writing was neater than this chicken scratch.

Keep breathing. Count your breaths if you have to. One day breathing won't be as difficult. One day you won't have to count. I promise, there is good stuff waiting for you. It will find you.

I reread it a few times. The advice was simple, but in its own unique way, quite powerful. Then suddenly, Mom and the lady from The Cove came back into the room. I flattened my hands over the card, hiding it against my chest. I didn't want anyone else reading it. And as this lady spoke, I mentally counted each breath. The counting thing seemed to help. And when she stopped talking, I decided I would give The Cove a chance. What did I have to lose? Maybe good could come from it.

Good *had* come from The Cove. It had been a safe place for me to grieve—away from all the added pressure and drama surrounding my life. But now that I was home, and now that the sting from my brother's death had turned into more of a dull ache, something else had come into focus—Noah. I hadn't known until now that he'd been the one to write those words, but I'd carried that card around with me for the past four months anyway.

Noah didn't *just* save me the night he'd stopped me from bleeding out. He'd done it one hundred times over since that night. Every time I felt trapped by my grief, unsure what the purpose of my life was, scared, or alone, I'd counted my breaths and reminded myself, even when I didn't believe myself, that good stuff *was* coming. And it had come. My roommate Patty had been the friend I'd needed while at The Cove, the counselors had taught me other coping methods, and time had helped heal some of the pain that once consumed me. I was even making progress with my family. And getting to spend this past week with Noah, falling in love with Noah—I now knew with absolute certainty that those words on his little card were true.

Even when you think all hope is lost, things *can* get better.

The only problem was…

I felt so undeserving of Noah.

As I waited for my parents to come home, and then ultimately go to bed, I considered marching downstairs and ending everything with him. After the shit I'd put my family through, why should I get to be with such an amazing guy? Why should I get to be happy? These were pessimistic thoughts, the very things I'd been taught by my counselors to dispute and push away, and I tried hard to ignore them. But I struggled, and I'd been struggling since I realized Noah had been the one to write those words on that little card.

Around eleven, I made up my mind and crept downstairs. All the lights in the house were out and because of the rain outside, it was especially dark tonight. I had to feel along the wall to find my way. Even if I didn't deserve Noah, there was no chance in hell I'd do anything to ruin what had started between us. I couldn't do that—not to him. Maybe he wasn't falling in love with me like I was with him, but I still knew he had strong feelings for me. The way he held me each night, the way he lingered when he kissed me, and the way he continuously made me feel safe—all of it told me he cared. *Really* cared. And I'd never purposely do anything that would hurt him.

Entering the room, my heart doing jumping jacks, I found the bedroom light on, emptiness, and the sound of the rain outside drizzling against the window.

"Georgie?"

It was Noah. I hadn't noticed him initially because he sat on the floor, out of view between the bed and the wall. "I didn't want anyone else to come in here and find me," he explained, standing. He wore his same clothes from earlier, not his pajamas. And instead of being fast asleep in bed, he was completely wide awake.

He'd been waiting up for me.

Exactly like he said he would.

He crossed the short distance that separated us and hugged me. I stood there, a little shocked by his sudden movement, and let him hold me. I was more nervous now than I'd ever been around him before. We'd had sex, in the broad daylight. He'd seen every inch of my skin. And vice versa. I shouldn't have felt all this acidic 'I-ate-rocks-for-dinner' churning in my stomach. But I did. I tried to break free of his embrace, but his strong arms wouldn't let me move.

"Noah," I insisted. "Please."

"No. Fucking hug me back, Georgie," he whispered, his voice gritty. "I need you to hug me back. For at least a moment."

"Fine." I moved my arms from where they were locked over my

stomach and squeezed them around his slim waist. Through the material of his shirt, I felt the warmth that he radiated and the lines of his hard muscles. The way I fit against him had already become very familiar—wonderfully familiar. I held onto him tight and something instantly changed inside me. This moment reminded me of that first night we'd snuggled in bed together—how initially I'd been rigid in his arms, but after a few minutes, I couldn't help when I'd relaxed into him. That same thing happened now. Whatever guard I had surrounding me like an iron wall—it dropped. Relief rushed over me, and I buried my face in his chest, inhaling deeply.

"There you are. Finally." He sighed, squeezing his arms around me tighter. "You had me going out of my damn mind waiting down here tonight." His fingers tangled into my hair, as if he wanted to hold me more firmly in place. Dropping his head to my shoulder, he dragged his mouth over my skin, kissing and nibbling. "I'm not very good at staying still when my mind is working like it does."

"You could have left," I suggested.

"No. I couldn't have." His grip loosened and he used his hands to brush my hair away from my ear. Then he whispered, his voice so low that it felt like a soft hum, "I fucked you in the sand this morning. And now I'm going to make love to you."

Holy shit. "Is there a difference?" I choked out, my throat clogging up on me.

"With anyone else? Yes. I'm certain of it. With you? I don't know. They might be one and the same." He scooped me up in his arms. Good thing too because my knees were about to give out, and he carried me to the side of the bed. He set me down on the carpet—in the spot he'd been sitting between the wall and the bed—and he began pulling everything off the bed.

He started arranging the pillows and blankets on the ground. I think he was creating a little nest or something. *Um? Was he scared that if we had sex on the waterbed we'd pop it?* Because why else would he go to so much trouble? I sat there, watching him and trying my best not to laugh. "What the hell are you doing?" I finally asked.

He stopped his incessant arranging and stared at me. "Getting comfortable," he answered, dead serious.

"On the floor?"

"The lock on this room doesn't work. What if someone comes downstairs to check on you? At least we'd have the bed to block us. I'm sure your mom really wants to see my ass."

I let out such a loud laugh that I had to smack my hand over my mouth to stifle it. "If I were my mom I'd totally want to see your ass," I joked. Flopping down in the middle of his cover creation, I stared up at him. "Just saying."

"Not funny," he groaned, giving me a stern face. "And stop messing up all my hard work."

"Like this?" I asked, wiggling on the sheets.

"Yes. Like that."

I stopped moving. "Earlier I said something about you *not being different*," I uttered. "And I need to take that back. Immediately. You *are* different—very different. And that's my favorite thing about you. It's all your different, weird Noah-isms that I can't get enough of."

He smiled, looking away from me for a moment and running his hand through his hair. Then his eyes came back to settle on mine. Damn, those eyes of his were going to ruin me. "Noah-isms? Don't tell Ellie that one or she'll use it daily." He sighed, inching closer to me, grabbing my legs and lifting them over his lap. His hands rested over my thighs. "I need to ask you something now, mostly because it's one of those things I need to know or it will drive me insane."

"Okay."

"Did Logan cheat on you?"

Heat crept up my neck. "Yes. What made you ask that?"

"Something you implied earlier." He shook his head, groaning and swearing under his breath.

Ugh. I wished he hadn't brought this up now. But either way, after my behavior earlier, I felt I owed him an explanation. "It happened about a month after we got together. I had a track meet or something and hadn't been at the same party he'd been at. He drank too much and ended up spending the night with another girl. I never asked who."

"But you forgave him?"

"Yes. I guess. I don't know. I forgave him, but I never really got over it. I think that's why when I saw you with Sydney earlier, I thought what happened with Logan was happening all over again. I know now that I was wrong. Like I said, you're different." I shrugged. "Can we stop talking about this? We were having such a good conversation before. And…well…I thought you were going to make love to me."

"I will." He smiled briefly. "Very soon." He shifted, and finally laid down beside me on our cover-nest-creation-thingy. "It's not really my business, but you shouldn't have put up with his shit. I don't understand how anyone could ever be distracted by someone else when they've got your attention. Only an asshole would give up on an amazing girl like you, Georgie. I mean that. And that won't be me. So if you see me talking with a girl, anywhere, know that I'm only *talking*. Come over and fucking say hi. Because I don't like conversations with ninety-nine point nine percent of people and most likely I'll be in need of your rescuing. Okay?"

I nodded, my skin burning a little too hot and my heart pounding a little too hard. Noah had a way of making me feel very cared for, very safe, very special…very *everything*. With him I was impervious to the rest of the world. And that was such a good feeling.

"I should have said hi," I whispered.

"You should have said hi," he repeated.

"I can't believe you asked me to be your girlfriend though. That was pretty unexpected. But I liked it." I smiled, turning and hiding against our shared pillow.

"Whatever," he said and cupped my face in his hands. He forced my eyes to stay on his as he inched a little closer. "What the hell ever. It's what I wanted." He took a deep breath, his hands on my face continuing to hold tight. "I'm going to make love to you now. I'm going to make you come and then I'm probably going to want to snuggle after."

Noah was so serious that I could only nod in response.

He stood, unexpectedly, leaving me. He moved across the room and flipped off the light. Black coated everything. My only company was the steady, soft sound of the rain as I waited in our little nest of blankets for him to find his way through the dark room and back to me.

It felt like an eternity ticked by, the eagerness of what was to come taking over every one of my senses—I couldn't wait for his touch, his smell, his taste. And then suddenly he was right there with me, lying beside me. His hands found their way to my hair. Tugging it tight, he drew me in closer against him…until my lips connected with his. His kiss was warm and thick with emotion. His tongue dipped into my mouth, meeting mine with a light touch.

I swear I forgot my own name. I forgot everything in the world that mattered and everything that didn't. I forgot that we were on a basement floor and that my parents were only two floors above us. I forgot the fears, the doubts, and the past. Instead, I gave in to Noah. He was the only thing that existed, and I wanted this moment to last forever.

His kiss was tender, but it grew and changed into something rougher, something that meant to claim. Suddenly, we were in a mad race to get each other's clothing off. I think when Noah said 'make love' he meant he wanted to go slow, but the pull between us was too powerful for that. There was a desperation, and it was impossible to fight. The same thing had happened on the sand. I'm certain he hadn't planned to take things as far as he did that first time. But, as sure as the stars in the sky, we had sex anyway. Just like it was going to happen now.

Too many layers of clothing blocked our way and we both moved to help each other undress. Pants, shirts, shorts, underwear—all of it gone in a matter of seconds. We were left skin against glorious skin, both of us breathing heavy. Noah took a new position on top of me, moving between my legs. His weight and warmth pinned me against the cotton covers, and I ran my fingers over the hard edges of his back. My eyes had adjusted some to the darkness. Faintly, I could see his handsome, strong face watching me—the want and need screaming in his eyes had me wiggling under his fine body.

He whispered my name and his hot mouth moved down to brush lightly across one of my breasts. My nipples puckered under his touch. "You're so beautiful. You drive me crazy," he uttered. His words warmed my already blazing skin more than even his mouth. "And I can't control myself with you." He sounded both bothered and excited by his own words. His tongue circle around one nipple and then he moved to do the same with the other. I held my breath as I watched. Swearing softly, he stopped for a moment and rested his forehead against my heaving chest. "And I love that I can't keep even a shred of control with you."

"Noah," I whispered. It was a plea.

"Yes?"

I couldn't comprehend much beyond the hot ache that had formed deep in my abdomen. I wanted more from him. I wanted him to lose himself in me like he had earlier this morning. "Don't stop," I managed. "Whatever you do, don't stop."

"I won't, Georgie. Not now. Not ever."

His mouth moved lower, down my body, kissing everywhere his lips made contact. Something intense was building under my skin, from his kisses alone, and I didn't think I'd ever get used to how easily he could affect me. It was a crazy-scary, crazy-good, crazy-intense feeling.

But then suddenly he pulled back—his big hands cupping under my thighs. He lifted me, moving me, positioning me closer to him. I couldn't see much through the darkness, so I couldn't tell what he was about to do. Earlier, on the beach, he'd surprised me. One moment I'd been without him, needy and waiting, and then the next thing I knew he was pressing his erection inside me, filling me as deep as he could go. Honestly, it had hurt a little. Noah had been gentle and slow initially, and it was the type of hurt that was the good kind of hurt, but he was bigger than what I was used to and it had taken me a few moments to adjust. Even now, I was still a tiny bit sore from our first time—like a reminder—and somehow that made me only want him more. I ached to feel him inside me again.

But instead of doing as I expected, I suddenly felt his hot open mouth against me. I gasped. I hadn't expected *that*. Of everything he could have done, I never really thought he'd do *that*. No guy had ever tasted me like this before. I didn't even know guys liked to do this. Part of me wanted to tell him to stop—I was too embarrassed. But the warm caress of his tongue and mouth, mimicking the soft yet hard way he kissed, had me doing nothing to end this. Instead, I arched my back and pressed into his mouth. Each stroke of his tongue forced me closer and closer to something I desperately needed to reach.

"Noah," I moaned. Actually, I might have purred and rocked against his face, but I can't be certain. I was too far beyond the point of embarrassment to care. The buildup inside me was too much. I rested my arms above my head. "Shit, Noah. Yes!"

At my words he stopped.

Swiftly he moved up my body and pressed one kiss to my lips. His thumb took the place of where his mouth had previously been. He stroked in the slowest, laziest, half-assed, but still amazing, little circles. I think he did this because he wanted to keep me close to my climax, but at the same time, he didn't want me to come yet either. "You've got to be quiet, baby," he whispered, his breath hot against my cheek. "Okay?" The painfully slow movement of his thumb continued. Now he was flat-out torturing me. "Next time we do this we'll be in my bed where you can be as loud as you want. Because there is nothing sweeter than hearing you say my name while I'm buried deep inside you. But for now you have to stay quiet. Promise me you will."

Stuck in some kind of erotic haze, I managed to choke out an, "I'll be quiet." My whole body tingled, and I was seconds away from combusting. It didn't matter how slowed he moved, I was going to come anyway.

Then, suddenly, he stopped moving all together and his touch left me. I would have cursed him, but something that wasn't his finger nudged against my very ready entrance. *Holy shit.* Our flesh was touching and I was breathing so hard, it felt as if I was running some kind of marathon. Noah didn't waste any more time. He kissed me hard, pressing his tongue inside my mouth, and at the very same moment, he thrust deep inside me. There was nothing slow or easy about the way he penetrated me. It was powerful. It was complete. It was life changing. And the very moment he slammed inside me, the orgasm I'd been hovering around hit my entire body like a wrecking ball.

It shattered me.

Electric wave after wonderful electric waved zapped through me. He withdrew and pumped deep inside me once more, and then he repeated this motion—again and again. I would have cried out, had I been capable of it, but Noah's mouth was still pressed to mine. He crushed his chest to my chest, unyielding in his strokes, as wonderful, perfect tremors continued to rock my body. My vision blurred as the muscles within me clutched hard around him.

"Fuck me," Noah swore, his mouth leaving mine so we could both breathe.

The moment lasted and lasted, until I couldn't take anymore.

I grabbed his tight, drool-worthy ass to stop his movements. My tremors were slowing, and I'd become too sensitive. I needed him to pause for a moment. He stilled, resting his forehead against mine.

"You okay?" he asked.

I'd turned into liquid goo under him, and I loved it. In this moment, I'd never felt closer to another human being. I'd never felt so wanted or so safe. I muttered something, but I didn't think whatever I said came out as actual words.

"I'm going to take that as a *yes*," he said and started to move again— slower this time.

chapter 19

NOAH

Fuck. I forgot a damn condom. Again. Something about her made something *very* primal about me roar to life. And when that happened, my brain stopped functioning properly. I'd been with several women over the years. I was no saint. I'd been with girls who liked sex slow and those who liked it fast, some who faked orgasms, some who I was certain didn't, some who liked it missionary, and those who liked it wilder.

Nobody compared to Georgie.

Nobody made me lose my mind like her.

Uttering every curse word in my vocabulary, I pulled out and moved for my pants. I found them and the single condom I'd pocketed earlier. Thinking I wouldn't cross the line and have sex in her parents' home, I'd nearly *not* brought any at all. But thankfully I'd changed my mind at the last second and had at least the one. Dammit. I already knew one wouldn't be nearly enough, so I was going to have to make this one count. But before I could put it on and finish what I'd started, the light in the room needed to be back on.

She was hard to see through the darkness, and I really wanted to see her. I flipped it on, and she automatically shielded her eyes. She lay, so gloriously naked, on the white sheets beneath where I stood. Her hair fanned the pillow and as she uncovered her face, her big blue eyes glared up at me.

"Sorry," I offered, but I wasn't sorry. "I needed to see you." Spotting my t-shirt on the edge of the stripped bed, I grabbed it and tossed it over the lamp shade. It dimmed the room somewhat. Then I stepped over her, ripped the packaging on the condom, and started to roll it over my length. Her eyes were far too alert and way too focused on the spot between my legs. It made such a simple thing difficult. And very erotic. Her laying there and watching me like that—my knees were going weak.

"Georgie," I whispered.

She sat up, her dark hair a wild mess around that pretty face, and she reached for me. Her small hand touched my bigger one. I froze. She was on her knees and right in front of me. She forced my hand to roll the condom in the opposite direction. It reached the head of my penis and dropped to the floor.

My throat felt dry and scratchy and for the life of me I couldn't move.

With the lightest touch, her fingers trailed over my skin. Then, my heart burning like the sun stuck inside my chest, she leaned her sweet body forward and those plump lips of hers kissed the tip. I nearly lost my shit. She pressed a second soft kiss there, while her wide eyes continued to stare straight up at me.

"I'm nervous, Noah," she muttered, her tongue taking a small lick. "I've never done this before."

Hell, I wouldn't be able to last ten seconds in her mouth. Not now. Not ever. Gripping her strong, little triceps, I pulled her up to her feet and against me. "Not now then. Let's save it for another night. There's no rush and I want back inside you anyway."

She nodded.

Laying her back down on our covers, I moved between her thighs and slowly entered her. My thrusts this time were steady and sure—the way waves crashing on a shore are steady and sure. Sex wasn't hurried. It wasn't frantic or desperate. I took my time and savored every moment.

I wasn't exactly sure how I managed to get my control back, but I did. If this were just about me getting off, I would have let her take me in her mouth. I wouldn't have cared how long I lasted or whether or not she enjoyed the moment. But I cared. That had always been the difference with her. I cared so fucking much it hurt.

My hands explored and caressed. My lips kissed and tasted. My eyes memorized. Sex with her—fast or slow—*was* making love. I knew that with certainty now, but really I'd known it all along. And when I brought her to an orgasm again, feeling her dig her fingers into my arms, arch her back, say my name, and struggle to keep quiet—only then did I let myself follow her over that edge.

But dammit, like the complete fool that I was, I'd once again forgotten the condom. *C'mon Noah! Do you have shit for brains?* I guess I did because nothing separated her from me. So much pleasure consumed me, eating me alive and spitting me back out, that I barely pulled out in time. This moment was just as intense as our first time on the beach. And everything was magnified by the way she watched me in awe—as if she'd never seen a man come on her skin before. Damn.

The energy drained from me. I wanted to collapse beside her on our covers, but the urge to help her get cleaned up was overwhelming. I gave her a small smile, a kiss on her thigh and then one on her lips, and quickly went for the bathroom. Taking my chances being naked out in the open, confident Georgie and I had been quiet enough not to wake the entire house, I found a washcloth in the linen closet and then ran it under warm water in the bathroom.

Coming back to the guestroom, I found her exactly as I'd left her. She said nothing as I dropped beside her and washed away the evidence of our lovemaking from her stomach. I folded the washcloth and next ran it between her legs. Wide, confused eyes stared at me. I guess no one had ever taken care of her after sex, which plain pissed me the hell off. I ignored the jealousy and anger that surged in me for a moment, set the washcloth on the desk with the lamp, and returned to make good on my promise to snuggle with her.

"You didn't have to do that," she whispered, a few far inches away from me.

"Yes, I did. Most of the things I do are things I *have* to do. Now come closer." I caught her waist and yanked her warm body in next to mine. She nuzzled against me. Her head rested on my chest and her leg hooked over my left thigh. It was damn nice. I listened to the rain and her soft breaths. She settled something in me I never knew needed settling. Only with her, I could relax in a way that wasn't possible for me before.

"Noah?" she asked. "You asleep?"

My eyes had drifted closed, but I wasn't ready for sleep. "No, not yet."

"How come you like to sleep on the right side? Always the right."

I let out a deep sigh, thinking over how to answer. I wanted to be completely honest but didn't want to scare her off either.

"Sorry," she whispered, noticing my hesitation. "Forget I asked you that. I'm sorry."

"No," I answered quickly. "Don't apologize. You can ask whatever. But it's one of those 'don't want to burden you with my shit' things. And it's not the right side of the bed I'm particular about it—it's the side closest to the door." I gripped her hand that rested on my chest, intertwining our fingers. It wasn't easy for me to talk about this. In fact, I'd never spoke to anyone about any of this. "I spent my high school years with my uncle. Did you know that?" I started.

"Um. Yes, I guess I did," she breathed, her voice slightly uneven. Shit. Two words into this conversation, and I could sense her fear. Or maybe she could sense mine and was responding to it. "I remember Ellie saying you lived with only him. I think she mentioned it after the first night you ate dinner at our house. I don't know. I was too young to remember anything else. But I do remember you ate dinner with us a lot back then. I thought you were both scary and handsome—like a vampire. Mostly, you confused me. Anyway, what does your uncle have to with which side of the bed you prefer?"

Georgie asked that last question so confidently that, frankly, it astonished the hell out me. She had to assume something awful happened—even complete strangers could smell that sort of thing on me a mile away. And yet, even if I was frightening her, she asked it anyway. I had no choice but to tell her everything I could.

"My uncle was a mean, physically abusive man. He drank most evenings. That meant I always slept with one eye open, fearful he might burst into my room and take his anger out on me. Once Ellie and I became friends, toward the end of my freshman year in high school, I started sleeping more nights in this room than I did in my room at his house. Your mom gave me my key when she found out Ellie was letting me stay here. Eventually I grew bigger and stronger than my uncle, more resilient to his words, and he lost his power over me. But I continued to sleep here more often than not because I still preferred it here."

She breathed in deeply and then slowly exhaled, her soft breath tickling my chest. I probably should have kept my mouth shut. I was sure I just terrified the shit out her. But still, word vomit, I continued talking, disclosing more than I ever had before. Even Ellie didn't know all this— not in as much detail, at least.

"I guess, no matter how many years pass, some small part of me still can't fully let all that shit go. My uncle died two years back, crashing his truck into a telephone pole while driving drunk. Go figure. But somewhere deep inside me, I still have a small irrational fear that he—or some axe-murder or whatever—might burst into my room at night. It's incredibly stupid. I know that. Anyway, so that first night you slept in the bed with me, I needed to be closer to the door. You know, in case my mean uncle's spirit tried to come through the door and hurt you. Or maybe one of those axe-murders."

I chuckled at my own lame joke, making light of all my unreasonable fears.

Georgie didn't laugh. Instead she sat straight up, turning to stare down at me. "You're sleeping closer to the door to protect me?" she asked. But it wasn't really a question, more of a statement.

"Yes."

She groaned and turned away from me. Her arms circled her legs and all I saw was her dark hair spilling down her bare, sexy-as-hell, back. But I couldn't think of how sexy she was now. Not when I'd upset her.

I was about to say something else, but she spoke again before I could. "What happened to your parents?" she demanded. Correction. Actually, she sounded more annoyed than upset.

"My dad took off before I was born," I answered, truthfully. "I never even knew his name. It was just me and my mom until around my sixth birthday. The few memories I have of Mom are all good memories. But something happened, something my grandma never got the chance to explain, and for some reason Mom took off, too. I lived with my grandma next. Memaw—that's what I called her. I was with her for seven years. She was kind of crazy but sweet. She had a stroke when I was in the seventh grade. I still visit her at her nursing home a few times a year. She's not mentally there anymore, but she gets excited to see me. So, yeah. Long story short—that's how I ended up living with my Uncle Joe."

She groaned. It was an angry, fierce little noise. "I'm so pissed," she muttered. She turned around to look at me again. Her blue eyes were beyond brutal as they connected with mine.

"Why?" I asked. "It was my childhood, not yours."

I sat up, wanting to touch her but refraining. Her body was trembling—that was how angry she was by all this. Angry on my behalf. I'd thought it before, but I knew it with certainty now—she was fierce as hell when she was heated. It was a turn on, despite the seriousness of our conversation, and I had to ignore the fact that we were both currently still naked.

"I just am," she huffed. "I'm pissed at your shitty uncle. At your parents. And at myself. I had a perfect childhood, and I don't think I've ever really appreciated that. One bad thing happened to me and I tried to kill myself. You've been through so much more."

Lightly I touched her back. "I'm okay."

"I know," she said softly, calming down some. "That's my point. Despite everything, you're sweet and kind and incredible. You're *good,* despite the bad. And I don't deserve you. Certainly not after what I put my family through."

My heart was pounding. I dipped my head against her shoulder. "Don't say shit like that, Georgie. You made one mistake. Mistakes happen. It's called being human. You didn't die. You're still here. *Okay?* You deserve me. And you can have me—all of me. There's something so special about you. It's why I can't stay away from you. It's why I'm here now. It's why I always want to be here. Don't say shit like that."

"Okay," she whispered, leaning into me. "I won't."

I didn't know if I'd made anything better, but as long as she remained close to me I took it as a good sign. She needed to start believing she actually *was* the amazing woman that I saw when I looked at her. I'd help her figure it out. No matter how long it took. And, once again, I had to ignore the fact that she was naked and how fucking sweet her hair smelled. I had to hold my breath—because I was trying to be supportive here and all

I kept doing was turning into a damn horn-dog every twelve seconds with her.

Her hand rested on my thigh. "Noah?"

"Yeah?"

Her fingers traced lightly against my skin, moving in an upward direction. "That protective thing you do with me...it's sexy."

Oh, God.

"Yeah?" I muttered.

"The 'sleeping closer to the door to protect me from any bad guys' thing is especially sexy," she continued. Her hand touched higher on my leg and for the smallest second brushed against my now fully-hard cock. Shit. Then her fingers moved in the opposite and much safer direction.

"Yeah?" I choked out again. It seemed I only had one word in my vocabulary.

Her touch trailed back up my thigh, my skin heating under her contact, and this time, as she moved higher, she connected with her target. Her small hand wrapped tight and sure around me. *"You're* sexy. I'm still trying to figure everything out. But before and after that, you can have me too. All of me."

A growl escaped my throat. Gripping her tiny waist, I easily lifted her and in a single swift motion brought her onto my lap. I knew then that neither of us would be getting any sleep tonight.

Perfectly. Fine. By. Me.

* * *

We had sex two more times that night. And the only reason we didn't reach number four was because I was too afraid she'd think of me as some sex-crazed mad-dog maniac who couldn't get enough. I guess I *was* a sex-crazed mad-dog maniac who couldn't get enough. But in my defense, she was impossible to resist. Especially when she seemed to be as hot for me as I was for her.

Over the next couple weeks we continued to hide our relationship from her parents. Mostly because I didn't want to give up our current sleeping arrangement. Was it so wrong that I wanted to hold her every night? To kiss her as much as I wanted. To discuss such intimate things with her—things I never knew I wanted to share before. We weren't even having sex in the basement room anymore. It only happened that one time, that one rainy night. The reason it stopped was because I didn't like the idea that her parents were always under the same roof. I told her that much too. She didn't seem to care either way and so we reserved our nights for snuggling only. Instead, we started having sex in my own room, in my own bed, in my own house. There had also been a few times in my office, in my car, and once more on the beach.

For the first time in my life, I was acting like a teenager—experiencing what I didn't have the chance to the first time around. And if this never stopped, it would be too soon.

Unlocking the basement door, I carefully let myself inside the Turner's house. Then I relocked the door behind me. It was after midnight. As much as I tried to keep our work schedules similar, it didn't always happen that way. Tonight I'd worked and she hadn't. A group of kids had pissed me off when they decided to play three consecutive rounds of miniature golf, taking their sweet-ass time, meaning I couldn't leave until they did. Finally, their moms had come to pick them up. So when I left work, I drove straight here.

Coming into the open basement living room, I found the bathroom light on. Georgie was more of a morning person rather than a night owl. Usually when I snuck into the house, I'd find her already curled up in bed. Seeing the light on—my stomach was in knots and my heart was racing. I rushed for the bathroom door. The worst case scenario flashed through my mind—red blood contrasting against the white tile—and I burst into the small bathroom.

Georgie let out a startled little yelp. "Noah! Privacy!" she snapped. My girl was completely fine, completely intact, sitting on the toilet.

I laughed, relieved. Sometimes I liked to piss her off a little just for the sake of pissing her off. I'd purposely peed in front her a couple times before. It always brought out this same, appalled reaction. But I'd never walked in on her in the bathroom, and I could tell she hated it.

"Hey, babe," I muttered. "I'm here."

"I can see that," she groaned. "Now go away."

"Can I have a kiss first?"

"No!"

I laughed, leaving the bathroom as quickly as I'd barged into it.

Shit. I was a lunatic, but I guess a small piece of me still feared she might try to take her own life again. It would take time for that feeling to go away completely inside me. I stood outside the bathroom door, waiting for her to finish. The toilet flushed, water ran at the sink, and the light went out. A moment later she was outside the door, smacking me as hard as she could in the chest. She was fired up, and it was sexy as fuck. I locked my arms around her and planted a kiss on her lips. She resisted me for about one second before she gave in and kissed me back, her tongue lightly connecting with mine. It sent shivers all through me. Even when we were apart for only a few hours, I always missed her.

"Hey," I muttered against her lips. "Sorry."

She moaned into my mouth, making my cock stir to life. But I'd learned how to ignore him while we were in her parents' home.

"Hey," she whispered back. "I just got my period. That's why I was in the bathroom so late. Good news, huh?"

I breathed in. I'd recently learned—after stressing and driving myself mad for almost two weeks—that Georgie was on birth control pills. She was responsible and mature, so I shouldn't have automatically assumed anything less. She'd been on the pill all along, but I'd never thought to ask, which was completely stupid and typical of me. We were getting better about using condoms, but since we hadn't used one the first few times, I'd been waiting to hear those words from her.

In truth, I actually really wanted kids. I'd never considered it before, but being with Georgie made me consider all sort of things I never would have. Having a little sassy, mini-me Georgie pitter-patter around our house one day, getting in trouble, sounded pretty perfect to me. But just because I was older and more ready for things like that didn't mean Georgie was. There were things I wanted for her first. Like college. Or a career if she wanted.

"As long as you're happy, I'm happy. Let's go to bed. I'm exhausted." Swooping her up, I carried her over my shoulder toward the waterbed. It was going to be difficult *not* to have my way with her tonight. Tomorrow was the big day. The day we were planning on telling her parents everything. The day our relationship became something open and legit. I didn't *need* anyone's approval, but I wanted theirs. Both Ellie and Rose had easily accepted us, but somehow I knew her parents would be harder to convince. It was Sunday tomorrow, so when Ellie and I went to church I might actually get down on my knees and fucking pray. Anything to help my chances. But even if her parents weren't one hundred percent on board, it wouldn't and couldn't change a damn thing. She was mine, and I was hers. Nothing else mattered.

chapter 20:

GEORGINA

I tossed and turned all night long. No matter what I did, I could not find a comfortable position. I'd never had this problem with Noah before.

"Stop wiggling, pretty girl," his gritty voice whispered. "You're rubbing up against me and turning me on." Noah tightened his arms around my middle and held me more firmly against him. He pressed warm, lingering kisses to my neck and shoulder. After a few moments, his movements slowed then stopped. I felt only soft, steady breaths against my skin. He'd fallen asleep. His limbs were heavy and hot over my body, but I didn't push him anywhere. The reassurance that he was there and completely *not* worried about tomorrow's impending doom helped some. Before I knew it, I drifted off with him.

In the morning, I woke to soft kisses moving carefully up my leg. The scratchy five o'clock shadow that seemed to permanently coat his jaw, no matter what time of day it was, tickled my skin. He moved higher and higher. The feel of his kisses, his warm hands, and his hot breath were all still so new and exciting—I ached and squirmed. The more time we spent together the more comfortable he was becoming at showing me all the facets of his personality. Noah was shy and quiet ninety-nine percent of the time, but get him behind closed doors, and he turned downright playful. But I had to stop him, immediately, before he took things too far. I worked my fingers into his hair and fisted my hands, forcing his eyes to focus on mine.

"Aren't you even the least bit worried about today?"

He smiled. Then he moved up my body to press a quick kiss my lips. "For once in my life—no." The water in the bed sloshed around a little as he climbed out. He reached two hands behind his head and yanked his t-shirt off.

Hot damn.

His chest wasn't something I'd ever be able to casually be in the same room with. I could only stare up at him from where I laid in bed. Grabbing his bag off the floor, the one he always kept in this room, he took out a fresh shirt and put on. He did the same thing next with his pajama pants. And if I thought watching him change his shirt was magical—watching him change the rest was equally so. My jaw dropped open. Noah didn't even so much as flinch every time he did this. And he sure as hell liked to do it often.

Once he crawled back in bed beside me and I recovered from my 'deer in headlights' syndrome, we finished our conversation. "It's going to be fine," he said. "No matter what your parents say or think—nothing changes."

I snuggled in closer to him. "I know."

He began drawing little circles on one of my arms. His light touch felt nice and easy, but he shocked me when he flipped my arm over and suddenly pressed his lips to my scar. Then he took my other arm and softly did the same. My heart raced harder now than it had during his little strip-tease moments ago. I cleared my throat but didn't know what to say.

His whiskey eyes connected with mine. Heat flashed across my cheeks. Because only vulnerability shined through those eyes of his as he stared at me for a moment. "I've been wanting to do that for a while," he admitted. "Georgie, I…"

"Yeah?"

He groaned. "I gotta go."

"Oh."

It was Sunday and even though he never flat-out told me what it was he did on Sundays, I was pretty sure he went to church. That seemed to fit him somehow.

"I'll be back in a few hours." He moved back out of bed and started gathering up all this belongings—including the backpack. I groaned because I didn't want him or his stuff to go anywhere. And it kind of felt like he was about to tell me something else moments ago. "Bye, sweetheart," he said and bent over to press one last kiss to my lips. Then he was gone.

* * *

My morning sucked. Flat-out sucked. Waiting was the worst.

I took a longer than usual shower and blow dried my hair. Lately I'd been letting it air dry instead, so this was more trouble than I was used to. Then I fussed over what to wear, burning as much time as I could as my anxiety grew. And as I sat on the floor in my room, carefully doing my makeup using my closet door mirror, Mom cracked open my door to check on me.

"What's going on, Georgie?" she asked. "Do you have a date or something?"

"Something like that."

"Okay," she said. I could tell she was curious and wanted to talk. But we'd be talking about everything soon enough anyway, so I didn't elaborate.

After I finished getting ready—ready for what, I wasn't exactly sure. The inevitable, I suppose. I had nothing to do. I paced around my room some, but that was boring. Then I came downstairs and ended up French braiding Rose's hair, but even after all that, Noah still wasn't back.

"Ugh!" I groaned out loud, smacking the couch.

"What time is this guy supposed to be here?" Mom asked from her laptop at the kitchen table. "Is he late?"

I glanced at the clock on the DVR. Nine thirty-two. Great. It was insanely early. "I have no idea when he'll be here," I admitted. "I may have to wait all day."

"How about you and Rose go for a walk on the beach? It's only supposed to reach seventy-eight today. Today might be the coolest morning all summer. Go walk."

I was pretty sure Noah wasn't going to show up for at least another hour or two, but was I ready to face the beach? Yes, actually. I think I was. "Okay," I decided, even though I was probably going to frizz my freshly finished hair. "Let's go, Rose."

"Do I have to?" she whined but was off the couch faster than even me.

"Yes," Mom answered for her.

"Fine. I'll babysit."

I shoved my sister's shoulder but didn't mind her joke. We walked down to the beach, and it was surprisingly easy. After all, it was only sand, air, and water. Noah and I had had sex on the beach our first time together, but this was my first visit to the exact spot where Ben and I had fought over a year ago. With Rose close beside me, we walked. But when I reached that very spot, I dropped straight to my knees, pulling my little sister to sit on the sand beside me.

"Sit here with me for a few minutes," I told her.

Ben had a grave. A nice tombstone with nice words in a nice graveyard. His casket held a few of his belongings—his favorite shirt, pictures, toys from when he was a kid—but it did not hold his body. They'd never found his body. He'd been out on a rescue mission, smack-dab in the middle of a horrible storm, and he'd fallen overboard. The search party combed the water and the shore for miles and miles off the coast of Malibu, California, but they never found even a trace of his remains. And when they pronounced him dead—part of me died too.

Digging my toes and fingers into the cool sand, I stared out at the Atlantic Ocean. Ben died on the other side of the country, in the Pacific Ocean. But the oceans were all connected, and they were all the same to me. His 'nice' tombstone and empty casket weren't his grave to me—the water was.

"I miss Ben," I whispered to Rose.

"Me too," she simply answered.

I didn't cry. Instead I watched the waves roll steadily over and over onto the shore. I thought about happier memories with my brother. I thought about how he used to wake me in the middle of night, drag me out here and make me hold a flashlight and bucket for him, as he ran around like a fool and tried to catch ghost crabs. And as creepy-crawly as I found those crabs—I loved that nothing would ever take those memories of my brother away.

A second later someone's arms wrapped around me. It was Ellie. She smelled clean and fresh—like men's shampoo and maybe even a trace of men's cologne. Her thin arms let me go, and she plopped down beside me. I was sandwiched between my two sisters. It was nice.

"Is church over already?" I asked, taking in the sight of her. She wore loose-fitting khaki pants, a collared shirt, and the biggest grin.

"Noah wanted to go alone today," she answered, shrugging. "I came here because there was no chance in hell I'd miss the show." She tapped her tan, satchel bag, purse-thingy she wore across her chest. "I brought my new camera."

I chuckled and turned my focus back out at the water.

"Can I take some pictures?" Rose asked, pleading. "Please? Right now."

"Okay." Ellie didn't even hesitate. She pulled out her brand new, *very* expensive camera and handed it over. I knew Rose wasn't about to purposely drop it in the sand, but I'm not sure I would have been as trusting as Ellie. But that was just Ellie's style—she never sweated the little stuff. "Knock yourself out, kiddo," my older sister told her. "Do you know how to use it?"

"Yeah. Duh. Who doesn't know how to use a camera?"

Rose stood up, walking off a few feet away, and started snapping pictures of random things.

"I was surprised I found you down here on the beach," Ellie commented, bumping her shoulder against mine. We both stared out at the water now. "I thought you were avoiding it."

How did she know that? I hadn't told anyone about my fight with Ben from way-back. "I was," I admitted. "But I felt like coming out here today."

"That's good. That's progress." She kicked off her flip-flops and dug her toes into the sand. "You know, sometimes I wonder how the fuck Ben managed to drown. He was like a fish. I swear he came out of Mom's stomach swimming. It kind of reminds you that Mother Nature doesn't play favorites and that the world is much bigger than us." She sighed. "Want to get in the water with me?"

"What?"

Ellie jumped up, taking hold of my hand and dragging me to my feet with her. "C'mon." Then she called out to Rose, "Take some pictures, Rosie! We're getting in—in our clothes!"

I didn't even have a moment to resist her. My sister had a firm grip on my hand, and she wasn't letting go. Yanking my arm, she pulled me toward the sea. I laughed the whole way as we ran and dove in. The very second cold touched me, a giant wave rolled over us—knocking both of us onto our asses. I went completely under. It was thrilling and scary all at once. And I'd missed this feeling. I'd grown up with the water, it was like second nature to me. And even if it had taken my brother's life, part of me still loved it and had missed it.

I popped my head free from the wave that had dragged us down, splashing my sister. "Seriously!" I shouted at her, not being serious at all. "I just spent an hour doing my hair for Noah!" I splashed her again.

She splashed me back. "Seriously," she mocked. "Haven't you noticed that Noah doesn't care how straight, frizzy, or wavy your hair is? He's obsessed with other parts of your body, like your tits—not your hair."

"I can't believe you just said that." I jumped on her, trying to push her head under. Like a buoy, she floated and wouldn't budge. I gave up after a few unsuccessful seconds and started wading my way through the water, walking back toward the shore.

"You know," Ellie said, following me out. "You have nothing to worry about today. Mom knows freaking everything. She's like a mind reader. I guarantee she already knows about you and Noah. You didn't need to do your hair for today."

I was sopping wet, water dripping off me everywhere with makeup probably running down my face. "No way."

"Yes way. She knew I liked girls even before I figured it out. She knew Ben was taking those community college courses even before he told anyone. Trust me, she already knows."

I swallowed that pill down. Ellie was probably right. But if that were the case, maybe I'd been stressing over nothing. Maybe I had nothing to worry about. Maybe my parents already knew about Noah and didn't even care.

Rose skipped up to us, stretching out her arm for Ellie to see some of the pictures she'd taken. "Those are getting framed," Ellie said in awe. "You're a pretty good photographer. Maybe when you get older you'll want to move to L.A. and follow around one of your celebrities, snapping pics of them."

"That's my dream." A smile filled Rose's face and then she flashed the camera at me for a quick second. "This one is cute too." It was an old photo—one of Noah and I. We were kissing.

"Holy shit." I wanted to grab the camera from her little hands but couldn't with my wet hands. "Let me see that. Hold still, Rosie."

She held still for me.

It was totally embarrassing and totally perfect. Noah and I were kissing in the middle of a crowded Chancy's. My face flushed seeing the picture and remembering the moment of our first kiss. "I want a copy of this photo," I whispered to no one in particular.

"Noah already made copies." Ellie shrugged. "We better go back to the house. Church will be over soon."

I walked behind the girls. The raw emotion in that picture—on not only my face, but on Noah's as well—was devastating. Devastating in a knock-you-off-your-feet kind of way. Devastating in a can't-feel-my-lips-because-my-body-was-tingling kind of way.

He loved me. I loved him.

The picture didn't lie.

And he had to have seen that too. Weeks ago. Because I remembered now that he'd already seen that picture—moments after it had been taken.

chapter **21:**

NOAH

I had to believe that today would be okay. Facing any other alternative wasn't an option. Her parents would accept me as her boyfriend, essentially accepting me into a family I already felt part of, and it was as simple as that.

Dressed in khaki shorts, a button up shirt, boat shoes (*fucking boat shoes!*), with my hair pulled back—I walked up the driveway to her house. I'd walked this way a million times before, but it was different today. It meant more today. It sure as fuck better not be my last time today.

Ellie surprised me when I found her in wet clothes, sitting on the bumper of her mom's car—smoking a damn cigarette. I hadn't seen that girl smoke since we were nineteen, and she'd had her first puff under the bleachers after one of Rhett's baseball games. She vowed then that she'd 'tried it once, knew it was gross, and would never do it again.'

She looked unsettled but smiled when she saw me staring at her.

"What the fuck are you doing?" I asked.

Her smile dropped as the cigarette dropped from her hand to the gravely-sand below her feet. Her flip-flop covered foot smudged it out and into the ground. "Don't tell my mom."

"Like I was going to tell your mom," I groaned. "What the fuck are you doing?" I repeated.

"Relieving some fucking stress. It's not a big deal, Noah. Don't make it into one." She stood from the car. "Let's go inside and get your whole *meet the boyfriend routine* over with."

"Tell me what's going on first," I said, my voice softer this time.

"Please."

Crickets. She didn't so much as say a word, and Ellie sure as shit loved to talk.

"Please," I repeated.

"Dammit, Noah. Fine. Someone—someone I didn't even know I'd ever speak to again called me this morning. Okay? And now I have drama with this person to worry about. And I'm not even going to tell you who because I don't feel like it right now. I'll take care of it. It was just startling to hear from this person after so long. That's all. It's always unsettling when someone from your past sneaks up on you. You know?"

I didn't know. I didn't know because I didn't know who she was talking about. An old girlfriend perhaps? Ellie had tons of those. "Will you tell me who this person is when you figure it all out?"

She nodded. "Yes. You know I can't keep a secret from you longer than five minutes. But today isn't my day or even my friend's day. It's yours and Georgie's day." She pointed at my feet. "Nice shoes, loser."

Rolling my eyes, we climbed the stairs and went inside her house. My stomach felt like it was down in the bottom of my boat shoes as we walked. We entered and—surprise, surprise—the whole damn family was sitting around the open living room and kitchen area. Rose muted the TV the second she saw me—because she knew as well as I did that this was about to be more entertaining than one of her shows.

Mr. and Mrs. Turner sat at the dining room table, eyes on their laptop, working on something that was probably work related. While Georgie sat across from them, semi-wet like her sister, eating a sandwich. Maybe Ellie had pushed her into the neighbor's pool or something. What the hell? Did I need to get revenge for my girl?

Georgie stopped eating when she saw me, setting her sandwich back on her plate, as her eyes connected with mine from across the room. Mrs.

Sarah Darlington

Turner glanced over her shoulder to see what she was looking at.

"Oh, there you are, Noah," she said. "Georgina has been waiting. Come sit down."

I swallowed hard. *Had Georgie already told her?* From the shell-shocked look on Georgie's face, I'd say the answer was no. I moved across the room, as instructed, and sat down in an open seat by my girl. Rose popped off the couch and grabbed another seat, while Ellie moved to stand at the kitchen counter, where she hovered.

I didn't know what to say, but I knew I needed to say something. My hand found Georgie's under the table, her skin was cold to the touch and her fingers were trembling slightly. I gave her hand a small squeeze, letting her know everything was going to be fine.

"I made up the rat story." The words tumbled out of my mouth. "There never was a rat on the loose at our house. I've never even seen a rat in my life. But I made up that story because I'm in love with your daughter." I'm not sure if I even knew I loved her until this very moment. But I realized I was—I was so fucking in love with her that sometimes it was impossible to breathe. So why not tell everyone the truth?

"When Georgie first got back from that recovery facility, I needed to be here and be closer to her. I didn't know what else to do so I made up that story knowing Ellie wouldn't sleep at our house because of it."

All eyes were big and staring intently at me. Wade Turner looked as if I just told him I shit on the carpet. Ellie and Rose were only excited with encouraging faces. Susan Turner's expression was unreadable. And I wasn't sure what Georgie thought, because I was far too nervous to look directly at her. But her fingers were still locked tight with mine under the table, so I took that as a good sign. With my free hand, I brushed a stray strand of my hair behind my ear and continued talking.

"I love her. I'm going to marry her one day. I'm going to take care of

197

her and provide for her and have babies with her. And in the fall, when she decides to go to college—because I kind of have the feeling that's what she'll ultimately do—then I'm going to follow her wherever she goes."

Jesus, I hadn't even thought all of this through. I glanced up at Ellie, afraid at what she might be thinking. She'd given up college the first time around for me. And now I wanted to follow her sister away from Kill Devil Hills, leaving her.

"Ellie can run our business on her own for a while. I'll come home to help on the weekends—because I know we worked hard to get where we are, and I don't want to jeopardize our hard work. But...if Georgie lets me...I'm going to want to be wherever she is. It's really that simple."

Georgie's hand slipped out of mine.

"That's cool," Ellie said, accepting like always. She winked at me. "You're a badass, Noah Clark. I love you. I'll take care of whatever for however long you need me to."

"Good," I said. "It is what I want."

I set my hands on the table, tapping them a couple times, staring at my girl. Suddenly this had nothing to do with the other people in the room and everything to do with only her. I just spilled my whole fucking heart, and I needed her to respond. Now.

She blew out a long, slow breath and then slowly inhaled. She repeated that process a couple times before saying a word. "I need to know something. Just one thing. What if I hadn't tried to commit suicide? What if I hadn't been bleeding on the floor, and you hadn't saved me? Would you still have fallen in love with me?" Her eyes finally came to meet mine—they were shiny with unshed tears.

"Yes."

There was no question in my mind. What was happening between us was inevitable. It would have happened no matter what.

"Maybe," I said, and I brushed her half-dried hair behind her shoulders so I could better see her beautiful face. "Maybe it would have taken me a little while longer to notice you or vice versa, but you and me—us—we would have happened just the same either way. It's not like I fell in love with you because of that. You were going through a hard time in your life, and I fell in love with you *during* that time. That's how I'm always going to remember this."

"I love you too," she whispered.

My heart squeezed as she said the words. "I know," I whispered, bringing my hands up to her face so I could hold her and keep her eyes on mine. I already knew she loved me. I could see it in her eyes when she looked at me, tasted it when she kissed me, and felt it when she made love to me. I was the luckiest son of bitch on the planet—but I already knew that. I knew it from the first night I held her tight in my arms.

"Thank you for saving me, Noah," she uttered. "I never have thanked you. Thank you."

"You don't have to thank me for that."

"Yes. I do. And I might do it again tomorrow and every day after that. Because I wouldn't be here without you."

I kissed her in front of the whole damn family. I couldn't *not* kiss her in that moment. We were like two force fields, drawn together and colliding. Her lips were warm and soft, sweet and salty from her tears. She wrapped her arms around my neck, sitting taller in her chair, pressing her chest hard into mine. And when her tongue slipped into my mouth, seeking out mine, and I tasted her—I'd never felt more complete in my life.

After another moment, her father cleared his throat, forcing our little make-out session at the table to come to an end. I glanced at each member of her family in turn. There wasn't a dry eye in the room, including my own eyes, and I knew then that her family had accepted me—accepted *us*.

It didn't matter if I was older then Georgie. That small fact was never even brought up.

"You're a good man, Noah," Mrs. Turner said, standing.

Wade chuckled to himself. "I've never even heard you speak this much." He returned to the laptop as if the last few moments never happened.

Rose popped up from the table and went back toward the couch.

"Want a turkey sandwich like Georgie's?" Mrs. Turner offered.

"I want one," Ellie said, answering before I could. "Please, Mom. Thanks." She moved from the counter to the table and sat beside her father. "What are you working on, Dad?"

"I'll take that sandwich," I told Georgie's mom. "Thank you."

Mrs. Turner made her way to the kitchen and stared gathering ingredients from the fridge.

I smiled, circling my arm around Georgie. She still had tears in her eyes. "I love you," I whispered into her ear, low so only she could hear me. "I meant what I said about marrying you and having babies with you one day. I hope you're okay with that. And I will follow you to school. I don't know if I'll enroll too or not, but I'll be there. I'll always be there."

She nestled closer into my side. I didn't know if we'd get to cuddle at night anymore—at least for the time being before she left for college—but I believed she'd be fine without me either way. "I'm going to hold you to all those things you said," she said. "Forever."

"Forever," I repeated.

EPILOGUE:
A FEW MONTHS LATER

GEORGIE

"Hot damn," Patty swore, her eyes on a figure down the hall. We'd just finished our very first English 101 class. We'd always talked about this day while we were away at The Cove together and now it was here. Our first day of college classes and our first day 'out in the real world.'

Patty was from a small farm town smack-dab in the middle of North Carolina, and I was from the Outer Banks. Relatively, two different worlds—even though we both grew up in the same state. Now we were both attending Luke University. And I couldn't be happier that fate had brought us back together. We were the same grade, had both finished our high school classes at The Cove, and now we were rooming together for our freshman year of college.

She looked healthy too. Not quite as skinny as I remembered from a few months ago, but I knew she still struggled with all her food issues daily. Food was something a person always needed to eat so it would be a lifelong struggle for Patty. The same way missing my brother would never fully subside in me.

"You didn't tell me he was gorgeous," Patty went on. "I want one."

She meant the handsome, blond-haired man standing only a few feet in front of us. He wore a leather jacket, t-shirt, and jeans—a motorcycle helmet under one arm and his shoulder-length hair pulled back at his neck.

He looked like trouble waiting to happen, but I knew otherwise. He was one of the kindest, gentlest, most protective men out there, and he was all mine.

"Oh, God, I hate you already," Sydney groaned at Patty. "Keep your panties on. He's not man-candy. He's a human being."

Sydney had ended up at Luke University, as well. We weren't exactly friends—yet. I found out twenty-four hours ago that she was living in the same dorm as me. Imagine that. And we even had a few classes together. Imagine that, too. I'd never really given her much of a chance in high school. Before Ben died and before I left, I wasn't the same person as I was today. I was too caught up in my own world, too worried about what other people thought of me, and honestly, I was kind of a bitch.

I wanted to give Sydney a chance now. She was feisty, and I liked that.

Something had also happened between her and Ben—maybe they'd only been friends or maybe they'd been more—but I was curious, and either way, I wanted to see if we could be friends, too. If she meant something to Ben then she meant something to me. And after all, college was the place for fresh starts, new beginnings, and then all that other stuff.

"Hi, Noah," I said in a low voice as I came up to him. My cheeks flushed.

Even after a few months of dating, he still had my heart screaming every time I saw him. It screamed now—but that was a good freaking thing. It let me know I was alive. *He* let me know I was alive. Every. Single. Day.

"How was your first class?" he asked, impervious to the world around him and the many female stares constantly thrown his way. I'd gotten used to it, and it didn't hurt that his eyes always stayed faithfully on mine.

"It was okay. The professor seemed nice. How about your first class?"

The handsome man before me already had his associate's degree. He'd had to get it a few years back—when he and Ellie first started their own business. Someone had to have to business sense in order to run their business. So that meant he was already in higher level classes than I was. It also meant he'd finish college about two years before I would. But he was here with me now, as I knew he would be in the future, and that was all that mattered.

"It was fine," he said, shrugging, as he picked me up. "Alright. I've played polite long enough. Bye, ladies," he shouted to my friends. "It's my turn with my girl now."

And, like the knight in shining armor that he was, Noah carried me out of the building, toward where he'd parked his motorcycle, and off into our own metaphorical sunset. It was going to be a good life with him, and I was beyond happy that I was going to get to *live* it.

THE END

(For now...)

67037933R00113

Made in the USA
Charleston, SC
02 February 2017